Surrender

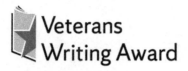
Veterans
Writing Award

Sponsored by the Institute for Veterans and Military Families and Syracuse University Press

In keeping with Syracuse University's longstanding commitment to serving the interests of veterans and their families, Syracuse University Press, in cooperation with the Institute for Veterans and Military Families (IVMF), established the Veterans Writing Award in 2019. The mission of the Veterans Writing Award is to recognize the contributions of veterans to the literary arts, shine a light on the multivalent veteran experience, and provide a platform for unrecognized military writers.

We invite unpublished, full-length manuscripts for consideration. This biennial contest alternates between fiction and nonfiction each award cycle. The award is open to US veterans and active duty personnel in any branch of the US military and their immediate family members. This includes spouses, domestic partners, siblings, parents, and children. We encourage women veteran writers, veterans of color, Native American veterans, LGBTQ veterans, and those who identify as having a disability to submit. Although work submitted for the contest need not be about direct military experience, we seek original voices and fresh perspectives that will expand and challenge readers' understanding of the lives of veterans and their families. Posthumous submissions are eligible.

Winners
2021
Surrender by Brian O'Hare

2019
Revolutions of All Colors: A Novel by Dewaine Farria
HONORABLE MENTION:
Mona Passage: A Novel by Thomas Bardenwerper

SURRENDER

Brian O'Hare

Syracuse University Press

Syracuse University Press
Syracuse, New York 13244-5290

All Rights Reserved

First Edition 2022

23   24   25   26   27   6   5   4   3   2

∞ The paper used in this publication meets the minimum requirements
of the American National Standard for Information Sciences—Permanence
of Paper for Printed Library Materials, ANSI Z39.48-1992.

For a listing of books published and distributed by Syracuse University Press,
visit https://press.syr.edu.

ISBN: 978-0-8156-1150-9 (hardcover)
978-0-8156-5573-2 (e-book)

Library of Congress Cataloging-in-Publication Data

Names: O'Hare, Brian (Author), author.
Title: Surrender / Brian O'Hare.
Description: First edition. | Syracuse, New York : Syracuse University Press,
2022. | "Sponsored by the Institute for Veterans and Military Families
and Syracuse University Press."
Identifiers: LCCN 2022026150 (print) | LCCN 2022026151 (ebook) | ISBN
9780815611509 (hardcover) | ISBN 9780815655732 (ebook)
Subjects: LCSH: Veterans—United States—Fiction. | Short
stories, American—21st century.
Classification: LCC PS3615.H3825 A6 2021 (print) | LCC PS3615.H3825
(ebook) | DDC 813/.6—dc23/eng/20220906
LC record available at https://lccn.loc.gov/2022026150
LC ebook record available at https://lccn.loc.gov/2022026151

Manufactured in the United States of America

To Johnny, Roderick, OE, Sweet Lew, Ed, Speed, Carl (Rest in Power!), and Jazzy—who changed the way I see the world

In the beginning was the myth.
—Hermann Hesse,
Peter Camenzind

Contents

Acknowledgments and Credits

Jim Krusoe—I know how much you hate being praised, so I take considerable risk in saying that without your wisdom and huge heart, this book simply would not be. The best teacher I've ever had. You truly give a shit, Jim. A rare quality. A rare man. I thank you.

Bob Mrazek—Congressman! I thank you for your wisdom, your tireless enthusiasm, and your bulletproof counsel. But most important, I thank you for your comradeship—that we're in this together. (And for your great face and for keeping my good bourbon safe.)

Andrei Konst—comrade! One of the best decisions I ever made was to give you a ride home from Venice late one Sunday night. Your O-1-Visa-level intelligence, brilliant insights, Siberian humor, and willingness to always have cawfee have enriched my life, and this book, in countless ways. спасибо БуБу!

Lieutenant Colonel Dave DiEugenio, USMC (Ret.)—one of the best human beings (and friends) on earth. Without your stellar creative problem solving, Buddha-like equanimity, and especially your armory of knowledge, containing everything I ever forgot about the Marines—this book would not happen. Semper Fi, *Consigliere*!

Tim Rhys—I thank you for your ancient friendship, and for your "Day One" belief. For all the laughs, the hard-won counsel, the blue-sky thinking, and the ever-flowing poetry. Never lose the hat! I toast: *Who is better than us?*

To 30B Writers Workshop, Santa Monica College—I am humbled by your collective talent, intelligence, and unerring instincts. But it is your love and compassion that move me most, your encouragement—for you, better than anyone, know how hard it is. Never quit! I thank you.

The Virginia Center for the Creative Arts—I thank you for your love, and for finding a home for me in your vast southern heart. (And for the Virginia Lightning, Paige Critcher!) One of the best places on earth for a writer. Here's to fifty more years!

To Kim Dower, my poet publicist. Though we've just begun our friendship, I am thrilled to have won your faith and trust. Your relentless positivity, intelligence, compassion, and tenacity make it easier to stare down the beasts. Much love and respect. Thank you.

To the Syracuse University Press and the Institute for Veterans and Military Families—I thank you for your dedicated support of veterans and for continuing the great tradition of the veteran voice in literature. My life was changed through the Veterans Writing Award. I'm forever indebted.

To Lisa Kuerbis, Deborah Manion, and Annette Wenda—I thank you for your professionalism, patience and good humor, your wise counsel, and, most important, your invaluable edits/efforts on behalf of *Surrender*. You have made this an infinitely better book. I am beyond grateful. Drinks are on me!

To Phil Klay—I thank you for your leadership, your unflinching love of humanity, in all its broken forms, and for your inspiration. Without you and *Redeployment* as guiding lights, *Surrender* might not exist. You are forever my map and compass—you lead the way. Semper Fi!

To Vasily Grossman and James Baldwin—wherever you are, thank you.

And finally, for Laura, Noelani, and Deaglan O'Hare—the loves of my life. The best human beings I know. Everything I do is merely an attempt to impress you.

Credits

The following stories appeared previously:

"Fuck Music," *Hobart*, October 17, 2020.

"Exiled," Liars' League, London, April 14, 2020.

"The Mail Thief," *War, Literature & the Arts: An International Journal of the Humanities* 33 (2021).

"Surrender," *Collateral* 5, no. 1 (2020); *fresh.ink*, November 22, 2021.

"Nothing Earth Shattering," *War, Literature & the Arts: An International Journal of the Humanities* 30 (2018); *Santa Fe Writers Project Quarterly*, no. 22 (2020); fresh.ink, October 7, 2020; *Bookends Review*, September 10, 2021.

"Sheepdogs," *Dead Mule School of Southern Literature*, January 1, 2021.

Surrender

Fuck Music

We're sitting in a pit. It's deep, well above our heads—a half-finished bunker, really, begun in the heady days when imagined snipers lurked behind every dune, when the sky itself inspired fear. But that was months ago—the war's over, and we're now merely bored. There's five of us: Montague, from a suburb outside Pittsburgh, reading aloud from Richard Wright's *Native Son*; Travis, one of the cooks, laughing his smoky laugh at something Gibbs said about his South Carolina hometown, "where the owls fuck the chickens." Harris, with his sleepy smile and forever unlit king-size cigarette, plays DJ on a knockoff Walkman while chefing chicken à la king, boiling in a canteen cup above an invisible flame.

Besides me—Francis Keane—Travis is the only white guy in the pit. He wants to hear Garth Brooks's "Much Too Young (to Feel This Damn Old)"—which could be any one of our theme songs. But Montague, not even looking up from his book, announces matter-of-factly: "Ain't *nobody* wanna hear Garth Brooks." Everyone laughs, even Travis. And that's that.

As lieutenant, I'm allegedly in charge. I use this bit of leverage to hand Harris a mixtape from Norma, my

1

jewelry-designer girlfriend back in Honolulu. Harris reads Norma's title aloud, written in ballpoint pen on the cassette: *Fuck Music*. He smiles, shaking his head appreciatively, holding the cassette for everyone to see, like a trophy. Harris pops the cassette, hits "play," dashes Tabasco from a small bottle onto his dinner. Horns cut the shit-talking—clean, like a blow from a butcher's cleaver. They herald the arrival of something serious, a '72 Lincoln Mark IV barreling down the Dan Ryan Expressway at three in the morning maybe, something undeniably American. We go silent as James Carr's "These Ain't Raindrops" fills our gut with bottomless longing, and we're transported, far from this hole in the Saudi desert, following an ancient yet familiar map of heartbreak. Around us, the desert night closes with startling finality, like curtains after a show. The song slowly fades. Travis's cigarette glows orange, making a small hiss as it burns; Harris's canteen cup bubbles contentedly. After a long moment, Harris breaks the silence, almost like an accusation:

"Damn, Lieutenant."

Homecoming

"Homecoming?"

Coach Auger grunted, his face pained, like he'd swallowed a razor blade. Humid teenagers ringed him on the AstroTurf, gray now in the autumn dusk. Some chewed mouth guards; others picked small bits of rubber from the turf, their faces ranging from adoration to boredom.

"In case you sugar cookies forgot, we got a *football game* Friday night. Don't get so distracted by Little Susie Rottencrotch and what she's got under her dress that you forget we got a game to play."

The boys looked at each other knowingly, pleased to be taken into Auger's masculine confidence. Auger huffed, passing a football from hand to hand, hopping from foot to foot like an agitated bird.

"Don't worry about a goddamn dance."

Quarterback Mike Donati, a big man in a small man's body, aimed his mouth guard accusingly at Ripley Montague, painfully tall, thin, and dark, a reluctance— the only Black kid at Deerfield High.

"Coach! Ripley's blushing!"

3

Auger squinted, examining Ripley's face with exaggerated interest: "You do look a shade *darker* than normal . . ."

The team erupted, howling like dingoes.

▲

Liddy Pisarczyk smiled, her braces dizzying and wonderful in the morning sun. She giggled self-consciously. "Homecoming . . . ?" Like she'd never heard of it before. Ripley nodded deliberately.

"You know. The dance."

Liddy lowered her head in thought, clutched her sweater. Lacoste's grinning alligator disappeared into her pale fist. Ripley felt the driveway tremble beneath his feet.

Ripley knew he was required to speak, to say something—but his mouth refused. The words vanished. His worst fears, normally tucked safely away in the basement of his subconscious, broke free into the formerly magic sunlight. Liddy's smile froze as she examined a crack in the driveway, struggling to appear both unconcerned and casual.

"I don't know, Ripley. I'd have to ask my dad."

With that, Liddy dug a chunk of asphalt out of the driveway with her moccasin and kicked it into the street. Ripley turned and stared vacantly down Pheasant Run Road, hoping for bus 7's speedy arrival and the deliverance it would bring.

Liddy wasn't at the bus stop the next morning—or the morning after that. And they avoided each other at school.

Ripley, and a pair of Pakistani twins, Azam and Azeem, sons of a plastic surgeon and a community college economics professor, totaled the entirety of Deerfield's nonwhite 0.3 percent. Three drops of color dissolving into a sea of nothingness.

Not that Deerfield was any more racist than the rest of America; they were simply oblivious. Their TV sets were their sole window onto Black America—you were either a Cosby, a Pittsburgh Steeler, or someone in handcuffs. Ripley Montague didn't fit any of these; he was just . . . *Ripley.*

Adding to their confusion was the fact that Ripley even seemed to *like* Mr. Burroughs's AP English class, lighting up at the mention of Brontë's *Wuthering Heights,* passionately denouncing Catherine's decision to marry Edgar, as a betrayal of true love to his slumbering classmates. Yet midway through such an outburst, Ripley would become aware of his thin brown arms waving and the octave leap in his voice, and would simply stop, midsentence, smiling blankly in the guilty silence.

The majority of the school was content to either indulge Ripley with a patronizing good humor (like when they'd commandeer Bobby Roberts, a wheelchair-bound freshman, for spontaneous wheelies down a crowded hallway) or simply ignore him altogether. Such is the luxury of the majority.

In time, Ripley came to accept this as normal, the price of admission. He wasn't a troublemaker or, god forbid, a rebel. Ripley wasn't even angry. He valued courtesy. Respected his elders. Was a loyal friend—everything that his father, a Marine in Vietnam, had instilled in him. He even took the Pledge of Allegiance seriously. And in the end, wasn't that what mattered?

As such, Ripley shunned the outsiders manning the school store, selling Twix bars and running personal errands for Mr. Dellavecchio, the store's faculty sponsor, for he was no outsider. As testament to Ripley's belief that he was like anyone else, just another Deerfield teenager, Ripley played football, that holiest of American pastimes. For there were no other sports in Western Pennsylvania—at least none that mattered. Basketball was a fine winter sport, but the appeal was mainly social, something to do until the ice melted. And soccer was for guys with pierced ears who wore OP shorts and Vans slip-ons without socks, even in winter, and listened to Devo—*soccer fags*, as Coach Auger put it.

So Friday nights found Ripley pacing the sidelines, his white socks stretched high, his uniform unblemished, close enough to the action to feel a part of things. Going into homecoming, with mighty Deerfield undefeated, Ripley had been on the field for exactly six downs. They'd even spelled his name wrong in the program, listing him as "Ridley."

Yet despite all the universe seemed to be saying, Ripley had faith—in himself, his friends, his school, and, by extension, in America and all that it promised. Not faith in the religious sense (though Ripley was not opposed to praying, especially for injury to Keane, the starting wide receiver) but a faith nurtured on the ignorance of youth, a kind of religion unto itself, capable of producing its own miracles.

Maybe that's why Ripley asked Liddy to homecoming—that faith. Somehow, Liddy seemed different. They'd shared the same school bus stop—the Pisarczyk driveway—for three years now. Standing together at the end of the drive where it met Pheasant Run Road, a gently curving suburban street of tasteful five-bedroom homes in the neo-colonial style, they awaited the arrival of bus 7 together, their proximity bringing with it a kind of intimacy. It was here Ripley felt free to gush over Brontë and his other literary heroes, Liddy introducing Ripley to Kerouac, Miller, and Bukowski. Baldwin even. Certainly nothing Mr. Burroughs would have approved of, authors suggestive of a rebellious spirit, who unapologetically rejected the middle class, Deerfield—America even—and saw lives lived on the fringe as the only refuge of sane men. It was as if Liddy saw something in Ripley that everyone else had overlooked, a hidden worth, the books they exchanged becoming a kind of communication, full of hidden meaning, riddles to be solved, transcending even the words written on their pages, through which Liddy shared the deepest part of her, a communion not unlike making love.

Even the light of those fall mornings urged Ripley forward, infusing everything with a shivering magic—where something as mundane as waiting for the school bus seemed somehow enchanted. The crystalline light revealed startling universes woven into Liddy's still summery hair—an endless spectrum of color running from melted butter to raw honeycomb, reminiscent of poolside days with golden friends, confident of their place in the world behind Ray Ban Wayfarers, the essence of

Coppertone, chlorine, and lip gloss simmering on their warm skin. And, as he looked at her on those cool mornings, it was all Ripley could do to not bury his face in Liddy's mass of hair, breathe deep, and savor her like a flower.

Ripley flirted cautiously at first, carefully gauging Liddy's reaction. She not only seemed not to mind, but flirted back. The hand placed on his arm, a playful punch on the shoulder, or, most thrillingly, the secret smile. In that smile, Liddy unself-consciously displayed the handiwork of her father, orthodontist of choice for Deerfield's youth, her teeth a charming tangle of metal and rubber. Ripley found in her smile everything that he was not. While his was a mask to hide behind, a shield with which to do battle, Liddy's smile, full and unafraid and confident, was an *invitation*. A collusion. Every touch, each contact with Liddy, however incidental, was seemingly from the hand of God herself—life itself.

Later, in panic, Ripley reviewed each incidence in his mind, as if gathering proof of Liddy's affections for a public reckoning of his heart. But this was mere evidence, a cold cataloging of facts and events, perception really. It was instinct, how Liddy looked at Ripley—as if she truly saw him—that consumed his thoughts. But how to explain that? The answer lay locked away in Liddy's pale-blue eyes, the color of the Delft china his mother used only for Thanksgiving, opened wide in real pleasure and understanding—a feeling impossible to put into words.

Why not ask Liddy to homecoming?

On Thursday morning, Liddy appeared at the end of her driveway as normal, bounding over to Ripley like any other October day and they were simply exchanging books. Her braces, wet with saliva, shimmered like summer pool water as she smiled.

"My dad says I can go to homecoming with you if you score a touchdown."

The words tumbled out fast, almost like a confession—as if she'd been rehearsing all the way from her door, a burden she couldn't wait to be free of. Those blue eyes, still bright and big, bore into Ripley as she caught her breath, full of the knowledge of her betrayal. He stared back, helpless, hoping he didn't look as foolish as he felt.

But even as the fairy-tale-like task imposed by Liddy's father sank in, Ripley couldn't get angry. (If that was, in fact, how he was supposed to feel.) If anything, he felt the thrill of possibility. She didn't say *no*, did she?

By afternoon, the news had spread. Ripley found himself a sudden celebrity—as if the ringmaster's spotlight had abruptly illuminated him, hiding in the shadows. Kids he didn't know, the lowliest freshmen, greasers, skin scabbed and cigarette burned, Emeric, the elfin exchange student who wore the same sweater everyday, tied about birdlike shoulders, like a gendarme's cape, even Mr. Dellavecchio, high-fived and slapped him on the back, as Ripley, smiling to no one in particular, navigated the white faces eyeballing him along his odyssey to the dubiously named "Nutrition Center," where he normally ate with Liddy in the corner by the jukebox. A hundred heads—*Hydra vulgaris*, Ripley remembered from Coach Auger's bio class—greeted him as he entered, followed by a standing ovation. Ripley smiled and waved, checking to see if Liddy might be waiting for him at their special table—it was empty.

He broke for the doors leading to the gym and the perceived safety of the bleachers, where Coach Auger let football players eat instead of suffering gym class. But as he entered, Mike Donati stood, his mouth stuffed with lunch, and saluted. Like the good Marine kid he was, Ripley came to attention, returned Donati's salute, then ducked into the football locker room, mercifully empty in the middle of the day. There he sat and ate, studying his playbook, mentally running pass routes in his mind, envisioning the feel of the ball, the soft braille of the leather on his sure hands, and the referee's upraised "touchdown" arms, the certainty of the gesture possessing an almost mathematical beauty for Ripley.

Coach Auger car-crashed the locker room, a sobbing freshman in tow, impossibly skinny in oversize gym shorts, cradling a bent pinky, surely a dodgeball mishap.

Like the Holy Father bestowing indulgences, Auger pronounced: "Study that playbook, young man. We score enough, I might just put you in. Get you some *cookie*." Ripley smiled self-consciously, feeling a drop of nervous perspiration run from hairless armpit down ladder-like ribs into the elastic of his underwear. The wailing freshman stopped and stared. Ripley ignored him, returning to the stapled pages in his hands.

Excitement whipped through Thursday's practice like leaves from the surrounding trees, fireballs of orange and yellow, a thrilling quickening. They debated dinner plans, whether a Chevy Blazer was better than a BMW for *Givin' the Dog a Bone* or if this mustache would get you served at Sudsy's, all of it making them feel grown up, like men, primed for *conquest*. Ripley chewed his mouth guard, feeling strangely detached, like when he'd had his appendix removed and was rushed into the operating room, floating on whatever they gave him, an ethereal river carrying him off to oblivion.

Thursday became Friday, the days indistinguishable. Ripley had had trouble sleeping, only adding to the feeling of a never-ending day. Liddy wasn't at the bus stop, but that wasn't unusual; the Lady White Tails had a "spirit breakfast" Friday mornings during football. As Ripley stumbled aboard bus 7, the driver, an unambiguous redhead everyone called "Fingers" because of missing pinky and ring fingers, looked up from the *Sports Illustrated* he read as he drove and announced: "Ain't no way that squaw's goin' to the dance with you."

The bus lurched into gear as Fingers hooted into the ceiling, the tarry laugh he normally reserved for bus fights. Ripley sat, ignoring Fingers, and smiled at the passing lawns, trying not to think of the game and the glare it would bring.

He could always join the Marines like his dad, right?

▲

Deerfield scored within forty seconds of their first possession. They'd hardly broken a sweat. Despite the touchdown, Coach Auger looked pained, testily reminding the boys they still had fifty-nine minutes to play, *plenty* of time to snatch defeat from the jaws of victory.

And then, timidly, just a few voices at first, the chanting began: *Rip-ley! Rip-ley!* followed by embarrassed laughter, trailing off as Deerfield lined up for the kickoff. Ripley paced the sidelines, nervously tugging his socks, stealing glances at the stands where he knew Liddy and the Lady White Tails sat. His teammates sought him out, leering and wagging fingers suggestively. Ripley returned their smiles before looking away, gulping greedy lungfuls of the popcorn and cigarette-perfumed fall air.

A football-loving God clearly had his money on Deerfield, granting four more touchdowns before the halftime gun fired, making it thirty-five to zip Deerfield. In the end zone, Liddy stood at the center of the Lady White Tails, a phalanx of red, white, and black, hidden behind her half-time smile, waiting—to go on; for the longest night of her life to be over.

▲

Auger marched into the locker room, finger upraised, as if firing warning shots into the ceiling. "You still got *two* quarters to play . . ." He stopped, a look of surprise on his face, frozen, an actor forgetting his lines. In the curious quiet, against the faraway thump of drums, Auger looked at the boys as they looked at him—the same boys he saw each morning, in cars, German, Italian, the odd American muscle car, driving to school, as he walked along the highway, sucking exhaust, alone. The look on Coach Auger's face wasn't surprise; it was *heartbreak*. Would they ever know?

After a long moment, Auger grimaced, as if resigning himself to something, and said, "Don't get cocky." But there was nothing behind it.

A pounding on the locker-room door, followed by squeals of *Ripley!*, brought an end to what remained of Auger's performance, like an oversized hook yanking a ham actor offstage. Running feet, and the laughter of those with everything to look forward to, gradually trailed off into the woods behind the visitor bleachers.

Auger went into his office and shut the door.

Ripley sat by himself, a family of ducks swimming in his stomach. Donati sat, wrapped an arm around Ripley, and giggled, nodding to the office and the closed door that sealed Auger inside. "Auger," he said, shaking his head. "What a *dick*."

Without warning, Donati grabbed Ripley in a joyous headlock, breathing into his ear: "If I throw it, you gonna catch it?" Donati squeezed Ripley tighter. "Right over number 37—Starcivec. Keane's been running all over that pussy, all night. You got it?"

"Got it," Ripley choked.

"Far right corner of the end zone. Right in front of the band fags and Lady White Twats. Right in front of *her*." Donati's refusal to use Liddy's name making her somehow more damnable, his revenge more righteous. "I'm puttin' it right on the numbers, Ripley. You better catch that fucker." He dropped Ripley, then stood and grabbed Keane by the neck, grinding their foreheads together.

"You fired up? I'm fired up!"

Ripley, his head buzzing, Donati's arm still hot on his neck, ran a gauntlet of laughter and faces, like someone escaping a grind show fun house, to the empty bathroom. Beelining for the stall at the far end, he flung open the door and fell to his knees, vomiting up the pregame pasta his mother made for him.

▲

The second half was a rout, a *crime scene* as declared later by the middle-aged men huddled over cigarettes and light beer in the Berteotti basement. Auger emptied the bench, unleashing a carnival of fumbles, missed tackles, and forgotten assignments. Visiting Monongahela even managed a wobbly field goal. Ripley paced, unbidden, seemingly cursed to walk the sidelines like a football Judas, until the Second Coming. As he marched, the many-headed Deerfield fandom followed Ripley, hungry. They'd come for a *show*—and began chanting, a demand now:

"Rip-ley! Rip-ley! Rip-ley!"

Even the tubas, like game-show horns mocking a losing contestant, joined in. Donati checked the clock: 2:24. He looked to Auger, arms outstretched, an accusation as much as a question.

"Jeez Louise," Auger huffed. "*Montague!*" Then turned his back on Donati.

Ripley's name rolled up the bleachers in a shiver, triggering what could only be described as a communal orgasm, an explosion of howls and trash filling the clear black sky. A cocktail of powerful chemicals flooded Ripley's brain, a kind of sympathetic orgasm, a pleasant speeding up and slowing down, where seemingly unrelated details—a heart drawn in ballpoint on Keane's forearm; the clean, almost antiseptic smell of the night air, signaling an early snow; that scoreboard numbers shaded more "fuchsia" than "red"—somehow all made *sense*. He presented himself to Auger.

"You ready to put somebody's dick in the dirt?"

"Sir?"

"You wanna play some football?"

"Yes, sir."

Yet Ripley stood fast. He turned to stare at Donati, waving him to the waiting huddle, and back at Auger, who looked as if he might be trying to swallow his chin. But something, Ripley's willingness to bear whatever indignity came next, a recognition or kinship maybe, disarmed Auger. He took hold of Ripley's face mask, almost tenderly.

"Son, you need to get some *dog* in you. Some *hound*."

Ripley stared at Coach Auger.

"You can't just stand here forever. Trust me."

And Ripley understood.

Not in his mind, that place of doubt and question, but in his *gut*—what some higher power, the football-loving God of Friday night, maybe, who made the drums beat, the lights shine, and inspired greatness, however fleeting—might call the soul. Something that couldn't be described by mere words. Leaning in, as if he'd been exposed, revealed too much already, Auger almost purred, "Well, then get your skinny brown ass in there."

Ripley loped to the huddle, smile fixed on his face. As they drew him in, Donati pointed at Ripley. "Just like we talked about. Far end zone corner—right in front of the band. In front of *her*. When you turn around, ball's gonna be right here."

Donati touched Ripley's chest. Maybe it was just the magic of Friday night on your opponent's forty with 2:24 left, but Donati's touch was electric. Ripley trembled.

"Right in the fucking numbers. You ready?" Ripley just smiled and nodded. The huddle broke with a clap. Ripley jogged to the far right side of the line where the Deerfield team stood, watching.

His eyes, opened wide in fear and trust, beheld Donati surveying the Monongahela defense. Across from him, Starcivec, the Monongahela defender, fixed Ripley with a predatory glare, his breath rising in powerful gusts, like small storms.

Donati took the snap, dropped back, and set up. Startled by the sudden movement, Ripley stumbled, then broke for Starcivec. Deerfield fans struggled for a better view, jostling one another like a mob at a public execution, not wanting to miss a thing.

Donati coolly waited, watching Ripley disappear downfield. Keane waved from the end zone—*he was open!* It took everything Donati had to not throw the ball—to take the easy touchdown. Donati dodged a Monongahela tackle, buying one last look at the field. Keane danced impatiently—knowing it was Ripley's moment—but *fuck!* He was *open!*

With agonizing slowness, as if running in a dream, Ripley finally crossed the goal line, turning to face Donati. Full of the confidence that lands crippled airliners, performs emergency surgery, and backflips into pools, Donati delivered a rifle shot, right between the numbers on Ripley's jersey, as advertised. All Ripley had to do was close his hands, hold on to the football. But the ball startled Ripley, Starcivec goring him like a hapless *Mozo* at Pamplona.

As he came to on the turf, Ripley's head winked pleasantly, like sunlight reflecting from Liddy's metallic smile. Tumbling away, the ball's stripes shone brilliant, blossoming hot and white in the stadium lights.

The Deerfield trainer, whom Donati called "Piggy" for his supposed resemblance to the *Lord of the Flies* character, crouched over Ripley, winded from the sudden physical activity. His face shone big and pink and bright in Ripley's face mask, like a sweaty moon.

"You okay, kid? Hell of a hit."

White flares, distress signals from a foundering ship, burned lazy arcs across Ripley's vision. "Liddy?"

Piggy made eyes at the ref, brows raised comically. "Liddy ain't here, big guy." His body shook with squeaky laughter. Ripley bolted upright.

"I'm okay." The ball rested nearby in the grass. He could just reach over and touch it if he wanted.

"Nah—war's over, soldier." Ripley grabbed hold of Piggy's meaty forearm and hobbled from the field. Disappointment rippled through the bleachers. It was official: homecoming was *ruined*. Thoughts turned to after the game; the beer stashed in the woods. The parties in three-car garages and finished basements, playing "thumper" and doing tap hits, while "Back in Black" rattled walls. The big dance.

The clock ticked.

Piggy's penlight shone painfully in Ripley's eyes, his pupils empty and black, like they'd been hole-punched, into paper. On-field confusion earned Deerfield a "too many men on the field" flag. Auger's clipboard sailed across the sidelines.

From somewhere far away, Ripley thought he heard his name.

"He's callin' you, kid," Piggy said, snapping his light off.

"Who?"

"You, kid. Better mosey." Head strobing, Ripley grabbed his helmet, pitching toward Auger on insubordinate legs. Auger, his arm outstretched, waiting, brought Ripley in close.

"You gonna visit?"

"Sir?"

"Me." Auger looked to see who might be listening. He leaned closer. "When you got kids. When I'm old."

Unsure whether this conversation was happening, or if some dreamlike consequence of his collision with Starcivec, Ripley replied, "Yes. Yessir."

"Let me ask you a question. Lunch—not a big a deal, right? Not all the time, just every once in a while. Hell, I'd even buy. A quick phone call, maybe, if they're too busy. 'Hey, Coach, how ya doin'?' That sort of thing. Christ, I'd be happy if they just honked and waved." Auger watched the clock, as if watching the seconds of his own life tick away, irretrievable, then shook his head.

"Ready to go, son?"

"Coach?"

"Homecoming. The goddamn dance. You ready?" Ripley just nodded. It was all he could do.

"Same play."

Ripley stared at Auger, jolted eyes shining.

"Jeez Louise, son. You wanna play football, or you wanna stand here with your dick in your hand?" Auger karate-chopped the field: *"Get!"*

The crowd roared approval. They were getting their show! With his thoughts still tumbling about in fragments, like mental shrapnel, Ripley carefully mouthed Auger's words: "Same play."

Donati swatted Ripley's ass and shoved him toward his position. As he set up, Ripley tried to ignore Starcivec, focusing instead on the thirty-seven yards separating him from the end zone. A lazy mist rose from the turf just beyond, disappearing into the stadium lights. Ripley followed the mists upward, to Brontë's Yorkshire moors, repeating to himself *Wuthering Heights rose above this silvery vapor*—as if invoking her divine intervention.

The collision of bodies jarred Ripley from his fog. Donati fell back, bouncing slightly as he set up. Ripley passed along the Deerfield sideline, close enough to touch. Donati held his ground, barely moving, waiting for Ripley to hit his mark, ready to unload.

The clock beat 1:30, 1:29, 1:28—a mechanical heart winding down; the end zone choked with players—waiting for Donati to throw. Waiting for Ripley.

The world blurred as Ripley ran, as if in transformation, conscious only of the sound of his chinstrap rattling against his helmet and his cheeks burning pleasantly in the fall air.

Liddy buried her face in her pompoms.

As he hit the end zone, Ripley did a tight turn, more pirouette than anything, graceful and agile, as he'd done a thousand times in his mind over the past week. Donati's arm snapped forward efficiently, like a firing pin hitting a bullet, launching the ball toward Ripley.

Later, when asked, Ripley would swear he actually heard the ball before he saw it—hissing sharply, the entire way, as if communicating with him. And on the ball itself, Ripley clearly read the name "Wilson," appearing and disappearing as it rotated in seemingly slow motion, the pebbled texture of the pigskin as big as the craters of the October moon.

Maybe it was just the concussion, but Ripley felt almost light, his movements effortless, the ball fitting naturally into his arms, as if meant to be there, just as he'd imagined it. And like he did it every game, Ripley simply handed the ball to the ref like it was no big deal, like he'd do it again, many times, and trotted off to be swarmed by his teammates.

▲

The Monday after homecoming, Ripley boarded the bus alone at the Pisarczyk driveway. Fingers didn't even look up from his magazine. He just shook his head.

Liddy wasn't at the bus stop that morning, or any other. Her father, the orthodontist, gave her rides to and from school until graduation. Liddy Pisarczyk didn't go to homecoming with Ripley Montague.

She didn't even go.

In time, Ripley and Liddy simply became invisible to one another, both dissolving into that sea of nothingness. But as Ripley took his usual seat and watched the empty lawns of Pheasant Run Road pass by, he realized something was different. Somehow.

A Communist Plot

Thinking back, I guess I just had a "punchable face." Or something. Certain guys just hated me. Like my dad.

To say we weren't close is an understatement. Like any boy, I'd fantasized about my dad and me going to ball games, camping, getting pizza, even murdering deer together during white-tail season. All that Norman Rockwell shit. I was even a Boy Scout for a few months until my Scoutmaster turned out to be a creep, personally checking to ensure all boys were "truly dry" after swimming in his backyard pool.

But my dad was always more interested in his Dodge dealership, playing golf at the municipal course, or hiding out in his sacred work room with his Johnnie Walker Black. He barely acknowledged me, beyond the occasional grunt or sarcastic brush-off.

▲

"A communist plot to undermine the youth of America . . ." is all my father said when I told him I'd made our high school soccer team, during an especially joyless family dinner. By his estimation, soccer wasn't even a sport, just a pastime for guys who couldn't hack it on the football field—losers with earrings, who wore eyeliner and had funny haircuts, "like that English band Devo." (Ha! Devo was from *Ohio*, Dad!) But at least he'd reacted.

Thus ended my "innocence," I guess you'd call it, my attempts to connect with the old man in any positive or wholesome way. Judging by the beaters my dad unloaded at his Dodge dealership, larceny has always been in our blood—so my descent into petty criminality shouldn't have surprised him. That fall, during a varsity football game, my buddy and I shot a flare onto the field from the road near the end zone. Coach Auger totally stroked out, watching his mouth breathers run around like they were under attack.

Like any good fascist dictator, Auger had his security apparatus, a sad little network of snitches and narcs, who ratted me and Francis out about the flare. He *knew* it was us, but couldn't prove it. But what really fried Auger's brain was that Francis Keane was like *Mister Deerfield*—National Honor Society, Reagan Teens, football cocaptain—all that white-savior rah-rah shit. If there'd been a "Future White-Collar Criminals of America" club at Deerfield, Francis would've been president. But Keane had an edge, a shred of something not totally repugnant, like his soul wasn't entirely dead. Like these pins he wore—"Gay John Wayne," the name of a band he wanted to start, and "Perry Como Gives Me a Boner," which is self-explanatory—on his varsity jacket, even though Principal Sabatini threatened to suspend him, because they were "disruptive." But when Keane dropped the big one, showed his real stuff, was when he quit football in the middle of the season. Auger had a total meltdown. It's almost as if he was in *love* with Francis, and couldn't believe he'd dumped him—*winningest coach in Western Pennsylvania!*—for *me*, so he chased after him; how Captain Ahab must've felt after Moby Dick bit off his leg.

Auger took his revenge in gym class, knife-handing us when we'd line up for "atomic dodgeball," barking: *Guilty!* He fucked with everyone but his darling football players, who, like reject walruses from some sad Sea World knockoff, lay fat and bloated on the bleachers, eating lunch and throwing tape balls at us.

One day, lined up along the basketball court, like political prisoners waiting to be shot, Auger blew his whistle, pointing at Keane's newly pierced ear: "Personal foul! Fifteen yards for unheterosexual conduct!"

In the eighties, straight guys just didn't pierce their ears. It took real balls. Francis was a ballsy guy, the only guy in school with an earring, a little gold dagger, a *vendetta* knife. Auger hated that earring. Smiling—if you can smile without lips—Auger tugged on Francis's earring. "Remind me: It's 'left is right and right is wrong' . . . ? An earring in your right ear means you're a 'peter puffer,' correct, Keane? Pardon my French . . ."

"*Tu as l'humour, toi! Suce un kloon ce matin?*" Francis chirped in sloppy French, which roughly translates to: "*You're funny! Did you blow a clown this morning?*" (Francis's family hosted an exchange student from Lyon freshman year; thusly he was megafluent in French cursing.) Auger jerked on Francis's earring, pulling him close, an almost embrace.

"What'd you say, Francis? Or is it *Francine?*"

"Sorry, Coach, I thought you said you spoke French."

"Why don't you and your girlfriend Dingle assume the 'Chinese thinking position'? On your faces . . . *now.*" He let go of Francis, flicking him like a stubborn booger. We dropped to the gym floor, dutifully propping onto our elbows and toes, chins resting in our hands, watching Auger strut about like Foghorn Leghorn on Adderall: "Shuttle runs. Line 'em up!" Tape balls rained down from the bleachers. Mike Donati, Deerfield's dwarfling quarterback, made a voice, cackling "Soccer fag! *Awwwak!*" like a drunk parrot.

Auger blew his whistle, imparting a "sense of urgency" as he called it, on the doughy teenagers. "You run like a bunch of *sugar cookies* . . . let's go! Pick up the pace." He smiled his lipless smile at me and Francis: "Having fun, piss-dicks?"

Sweat beaded on Francis's pale forehead, sparkling and freckled under the gym lights. His hair wilted, the gel softening, running down his scalp in sticky rivulets. It smelled sweet, like melted candy.

"Tons o' fun. Pointless discipline gets me *erect.*" Francis air-humped the gym floor. "I think . . . I'm gonna . . . ejaculate!" His face twisted, howling, "I love you, Coach Augerrr . . . ," then collapsed into a ball, and fake sobbed. Even the football players, who wanted to dismember Francis for quitting, laughed their udders off.

Auger nodded soberly, as if considering some particularly good life advice, a hot stock tip, or the secret to cooking a perfect medium-rare steak. With the apparatus of autocratic control crumbling about him, Auger crouched beside Francis, surprisingly calm, a regular Shaolin monk, considering. He leaned in, hissing in Francis's ear, "Someday you're gonna be old. And your earring and your 'bright future' and your smart mouth aren't gonna mean shit. And then you'll see what it's like. And I'm gonna laugh."

He blew his whistle.

▲

I've forgotten whose idea it was, who gets credit. At first, I insisted that it was my idea, because I've got a huge ego and I loved Devo. Francis was always more of a "Gay John Wayne" or "Perry Como" guy. (*Ha!*) Ultimately, it didn't matter.

Our beloved Deerfield White Tails were seven and O going into homecoming. Those head-trauma cases were even ranked *numero uno* on *USA Today*'s "Super 25" listing of top high school football teams; everyone was super jazzed. I felt like committing *seppuku*. ESPN even sent a crew to cover the game at White Tail stadium, our AstroTurfed temple to All-American violence, like ye olde gladiator fights at Rome's Colosseum, only repackaged for Reagan's America.

Of course, my old man's precious Dodge dealership dumped a bunch of money to fund the turf, a giant "Dingle Dodge" logo splashed across the fifty-yard line for everyone to *ooh* and *aah* over. Everyone thought my dad was a great guy for doing that for the kids, but I knew he was only marking his territory, like a stray dog pissing on a fence. The guy *hated* kids.

We didn't even have to break into the maintenance shed. From my stint as Mr. Oslawski's assistant, part of something called "Beyond Detention," for incorrigibles like me, I had keys that got me in anywhere on campus. Mr. O was the school janitor. I'd only used the keys a few times before, liberating the school store after hours, helping myself to whatever candy and cash those losers left behind. But this Thursday, the night before the "big game," when Deerfield's football players, those blessed bags of meat, were digesting pregame feeds, we walked right in.

The shed had a musky funk that was oddly comforting, a mineral-y tang of motor oil, water damage, and mildewed grass. The only light came through one murky window, from emergency lights mounted on poles around the field. It was the kind of place Stasi, the East German secret police, might interrogate prisoners.

"Check this out . . ."

I clicked on my flashlight, left over from my Boy Scout sentence, digging behind a pile of wheeled trash cans. In triumph, I hummed Wagner's "Ride of the Valkyries" from *Apocalypse Now*.

"*Duh-di-da-duh-duh, Duh-di-da-duh-duh, duh DUH!*" I circled Francis's head with a mostly full handle of Kentucky Deluxe whiskey, like one of the helos in the movie, swooping in to secure the beach for surfing. "Good old

Mr. O! Guy spends most of the day completely shitfaced. That's why he sings when he mops." I unscrewed the cap and inhaled, savoring the aroma, like I'd seen my dad, the ultimate bourgeois pig, do with expensive wine: "Mmmm. French fries and hot girl armpits—*Liddy Pisarczyk*." I upended the bottle.

"Gimme that." Francis grabbed the bottle from my hand.

"Whoa, there! Wait your turn, pal. You got the makings of a serious drinking problem. Mr. Dingle's a big drunk, so I'm an expert."

Francis tanked up like a pro, wiping his mouth on the sleeve of his varsity jacket. He held up a dented paint can. "This what we're looking for?" he asked, burping thoughtfully.

"No, dumbass. That's stain. For floors. Water based. Just washes away. We're using this." I slapped a shaky pyramid of paint cans, like one of my dad's salesmen unloading a beater. "Oil-based paint. Remember when we were at Thorsten's house and we put all his dad's liquor into a bucket and drank it? It's like that, but with caustic chemicals. We mix it together. This shit will literally dissolve AstroTurf. Try to not get it on your skin." I nodded to a stack of paint rollers on mop handles. "Get to work, Marine."

▲

We painted through the night, our magnum opus, a goulash of clashing reds and blacks and shades of institutional gray, leftovers from painting jobs of yore. We had ground to cover, roughly from the forty-yard line to the forty-yard line, across the giant White Tail deer head and my dad's "Dingle Dodge" logo, bang on the fifty-yard line.

Sometime later, I lit a cigarette heisted from mom's purse and surveyed our progress: two letters, a big, confident *D* and a less confident *E*, both maybe fifty feet high, ran from hash mark to hash mark across the middle of the field.

"This sucks. I'm drunk."

"Where's your 'can-do' spirit, Francis? Are you an Amer-i-*can*? Or an Amer-i-*can't*?" I nodded to the cans littering the field. "Back to battle stations," and I flicked the still burning butt onto the turf.

During the night, we got spooked, thought we heard noises, angry voices, the crackle of a police radio, the hammer cocking on a revolver even, but of course we were half-polluted on Mr. O's Kentucky Deluxe by then—and punchy from fatigue. Finally, somewhere in the vicinity of dawn, we completed our task, linking at the letter *O*. We dropped our rollers and shook numb, cramped hands, striking old-timey poses, Kentucky Deluxe raised in toast, like we were taking a picture commemorating the meeting of East and West at the completion of the transcontinental railroad, only of felony vandalism.

"Nice work, Francis, old geez! A direct hit."

While ugly hangovers stirred awake, we climbed the bleachers, where we could fully appreciate our work. From the East, toward Dingle Dodge and the "Steel City Mile of Cars," a kaleidoscope of sunlight exploded from behind the Alleghenies, which I took to be a kind of divine validation, erasing the night gloom. We could now see the municipal golf course, my father's domain, smelled the dewy greens and the fresh goodness of the late-fall earth. Behind us, in Deerfield Woods, tasteful five-bedroom homes in the neocolonial style, lights began to appear in windows, as the news anchors, corporate lawyers, and investment bankers began their daily conquest, with a good, strong cup of coffee and a stirring bowel movement.

Below, spread out before us on my dad's million-dollar turf, lay our own conquest, our testament to the resilience of the human spirit: the name DEVO spelled out in a fistfight of color, splashed across the fifty-yard line, surrounded by paint cans and that empty handle of Kentucky Deluxe, a "dead soldier," as Francis solemnly pointed out, as well as various broken rollers and trash associated with artistic creation. And it was beautiful.

With laudable Protestant work ethic, we heard the first ESPN van arrive, bright and early, the stadium parking lot still covered in sparkly night frost. I clapped Francis on the back.

"Time to boogie, old bean . . ."

▲

Though the field looked like the aftermath of an emergency appendectomy, the game went on. (In case you're wondering, Deerfield won, 3–2. *Yawn.*) ESPN moaned about the sorry state of America's youth. Local news haircut and Deerfield resident Don Cannonade even mentioned it on air—wasted, of course. The country was clearly going to hell.

We didn't even get expelled. Francis's father, a big swinging-dick construction-company owner, with corporate lawyers out the wazoo, threatened a legal hurt on the school if they fucked with us beyond a three-day suspension. Auger? That misery ignored us, pretended that we were invisible. But whenever he saw Francis, he'd unsmile and look away, jingling the coins in his pocket, as if to keep his hands occupied, so he didn't choke Francis or beg him to come back. The best part was that we didn't have to go to gym class—ever. My father stopped speaking or even acknowledging that I was alive, fatally short-circuiting what little communication we did have. He just spent more time pushing cars at Dingle Dodge, working on his short game, or locked away in his work room.

Fucker never said a word.

Aloha Friday

We were twenty-one. We could drive, vote, and drink—even invade a foreign shore if called upon to do so. Everything we'd ever attempted had been a raging success—we were captains of sports teams, class presidents, valedictorians. We'd been told we were the "cream of our generation." The best of America. And, young fools that we were, we believed every word of it.

There were twenty of us, midshipmen fresh from the US Naval Academy, let loose on summer cruise, flung to the far ends of the empire to train with fleet Navy and Marine Corps units. As if further proof of our sainted lives, we ended up at Camp Pendleton, with its palm trees and seventeen miles of beaches, just north of San Diego.

One Friday morning, after a ten-mile "forced march" ranging the rattlesnake hills of Pendleton, our officer in charge, Major Dillon, a graying beach boy, promised us an "Aloha Friday," something he said was a Hawaii Marine tradition where you ditched work at noon and fucked off to the beach to drink beer and play volleyball.

Two AAVs, or "Assault Amphibious Vehicles," hunkered in the bright sand, hulking and homely, like nesting walruses. Atop "Swamp Thing," stenciled in black along the nose of the vehicle, squatted a rangy white corporal, wearing gas-station sunglasses and smoking a cigarette, like an anthropomorphized rat in an old cartoon scheming to raid a cheese store. Even in that magic California sunlight, which made everyone look like movie stars, his skin glowed a dull yellow, his cigarette just another bad habit. The corporal took a final drag, flipped the butt onto the beach, and stood.

"All right, gents. Let's get the party started. Pair up . . ."

I saw Stark standing in the thin band of shade running alongside Swamp Thing, arms crossed impressively, his lucky Wayfarer sunglasses perched atop his spikey blond head.

"Hey, you big barbarian . . . ," I called to Stark, an inside joke after we'd watched *Conan the Barbarian* together. "You lookin' for a friend?" I waved him over. "Me and you, buddy."

Built like a slaughtered pig, Stark was an undeniably intimidating presence, but in a not-threatening, almost "cartoony" way—like something, well, out of a movie. Stark was even a math major, who'd memorized the first hundred digits of pi, whose smile, big and goofy and eager to please, negated all that implied menace. And on the inside too, Stark was all marshmallow, overflowing with easily hurt feelings that we never tired of trampling.

▲

The corporal watched as we dropped from the AAV deck into the rear hatch, a small compartment with benches where Marines rode, as comfortable as it sounds. Once inside, we stared up at him, standing above us like the crypt keeper or dungeon master. I finally spoke up.

"Major Dillon said we'd be doing 'Aloha Friday.' Know anything about that?"

"'Aloha Friday'?" He almost sneered. "Ain't no 'Aloha Friday' on Pendleton, Midshipman." We looked at one other, making *we're getting fucked* sounds. With a nod of the corporal's head, the AAV awoke in a belch of black smoke. "Y'all lose your lunch, y'all clean it. That's my rule. Them's plastic bags in back. I ain't nobody's maid."

He signaled to the driver, and the roof doors slammed shut, putting an end to the discussion, the hatch going black. The engine gunned and we lurched forward, racing across the beach like a circus pig into a swimming pool. We hit the surf and bullied through the waves.

▲

The engine cut. The Pacific slapped lazily against the hull, making peaceful noises, as if we were lounging inside a thirty-ton bathtub. The roof opened with a metallic groan, flooding the hatch with sunlight. We shrank back, hiding our eyes, like prisoners released from solitary. The corporal stood above us, shaking his head.

"End of the line, gents." He checked his watch. "I got Padres tickets, so 'chop chop.'"

We emerged into the white light. The beach just a thin line on the horizon, mere wishful thinking, blurring with the freeway and the scrub mountains beyond. Everywhere else: water.

"Y'all goin' swimmin'," he snorted, letting it sink in. "Major Dillon's orders."

▲

Stark and I treaded water, watching the AAV make for shore in a smudge of black.

"Fuck Major Dillon. Fucker ambushed us," Stark huffed. The AAV was just a noisy blur, disappearing beyond the limits of my nearsightedness.

"See anybody?" I asked hopefully.

Stark eyeballed the water, his flattop wilting. "Nope. Goddamn glasses are back at the barracks."

"Well, let's get on with it." I spit a mouthful of sea-water and launched into a graceless breaststroke, rising on the swell of a wave and then sliding back down again, going nowhere. The ocean clearly wasn't going to make it easy. Stark trailed close behind, a duckling afraid to lose sight of mama. I kicked at him.

"Back off, barbarian. I should've paired up with Reyes or Cornell, one of the water-polo players. Not your non-swimming ass."

"Yeah, well . . . looks like we're stuck with each other." Stark smiled his biggest kiss-ass smile.

Above us, the sun slid slowly west, utterly disinterested. We plugged on.

The ocean shifted, almost imperceptibly, more of a feeling than anything—the tide changing, maybe, in obedience to the appearance of the moon, dull and remote in the afternoon light, like an ice chip. A swell, undeniably bigger than the others, rose up. Stark tumbled into a trough, disappearing behind the crest. It's not just that the waves were bigger; the troughs were deeper too, more like holes—I was digging more than swimming.

Stark reappeared, chugging forward like some land-based mammal unexpectedly finding itself adrift, an anteater or an aardvark, maybe, his breaststroke more of a dog paddle. For a moment, all we could see was water, green and unforgiving, above us, around us, on all sides—like a cell, the entirety of our world. Stark slipped under, came up coughing, his shades gone.

"Goddamnit."

"They're just sunglasses. Ugly ones."

Stark ignored me, struggling to stay afloat. "This is kickin' my ass, Francis." Snot ran from his nose.

"Remember 'drown proofing'? From PE?" I took a breath, placed my head under the water, allowing my back to rise up, like the shell of some giant sea turtle breaking the surface. I pulled my knees gently to my chest. Theoretically, you could do this for hours, days even, until help arrived. My body relaxed. It was quiet and peaceful under there. Across from me, Stark grabbed water, legs churning as if to run away. I lifted my head, almost reluctant to leave my calm undersea world.

"See? It's easy. Try it . . ."

Stark took a deep breath, forced his head under and came up choking. "I don't like to put my head under the water. Okay?" As he said this, he reached for my arm. I eased back from him.

"You're okay. Trust me."

Stark paddled toward me, mouth locked in a tight grin, the smile of a rabid dog. I backed away, cautioning, "Hey, man. Easy." A swell shot past, catching us by surprise—and then he was on top of me.

We went under.

Stark clung to me in a mad hug, his arms like wrenches, twisting my head. I clawed his face, felt my nails dig into his skin. Stark grunted, the sound bent into a choked howl. He shoved me and I jerked free, kicking to the surface. Stark exploded from the water, sputtering. The tendons of his neck were drawn tight, like a racehorse straining to cross a finish line. His cheek was torn and bleeding. I pushed away, keeping Stark in view, stealing a look toward shore, still far off, still just wishful thinking. Stark struggled toward me, grabbing and desperate. I kicked him hard.

"Relax, okay?"

Stark spit, stunned into contrition.

The next swell hit without warning. I felt like I'd been sucker punched, tumbling, a doomed trapeze artist, headed for the sawdust. My face hit sand, grating against my cheek as I was snatched back, to the very pit of the ocean, where all was quiet and cold. And as I was dragged away, what I felt was *humiliation*. Who did I think I was?

And then, as if bored, the undertow released me; the water was silent, gentle even, almost feminine—a rebirth. I rose slowly, afraid to move, surrendering to the ocean, allowing it to lift me until finally, I broke the surface. A terrible darkness, without sound or form overcame me, as if being devoured—another wave, bigger than the rest. I ducked beneath this time, watching it hit above me, throbbing as it rolled toward shore. I emerged, gasping, the ocean still. I was alone.

▲

I crawled to the beach, collapsing onto the hard sand, for what seemed like a long time, half-expecting Stark to appear above me, his smile filling the California sky, dripping seawater.

He never showed.

Eventually, I got up to make the long walk back to the barracks, throwing my boots into the scrub, a kind of protest. But against who? Or what? I felt the blood pulsing in my veins, sharp and aware and connected to everything around me. The asphalt under my feet burned. A hummingbird startled past, hovering briefly. The air smelled unfamiliar, of warm dirt and desert flowers I'd never noticed. Even the sunlight seemed different, exploding off broken glass like a string of firecrackers.

A train passed; the Surfliner, on its way to San Diego, late sun winking off silver skin, windows full of Friday faces devouring the beach before it disappeared, rushing by in a dream. A boy waved, as if he recognized me. I waved back.

Okinawa

Brawley manifests out of the 4:00 a.m. dread, a one-man universe, his face silver and luminous in the Okinawa dawn as rain spits on us.

"Good morning, Señor."

Brawley salutes flawlessly and holds it, every inch a "recruiting poster" Marine, his ever-present dip already inserted. "All Devil Dogs present and accounted for."

Brawley often calls me "Señor" when we were out of earshot of the junior Marines, or were drinking, which is often. In return, I call him "Carl." This is technically against regulations, "fraternization," as the Marine Crops would call it, but I don't care. Carl is my best friend in the battalion. My brick wall. I return his salute, attempting to match his casual precision—and fail. We study one another.

"Thank you, Staff Sergeant." My arm snaps back to my side. My head throbs. "Fuck. I am still drunk."

Brawley wheezes. Spits. "The whole battalion is. Colonel just puked in the bushes." That's Colonel Madigan, our battalion commander. He's like a Catholic bishop or a capo, a mob boss, a ring to be kissed. Christmas Eve, I saw him alone at Club Ginza, dead Bud Lites surrounding him, watching Japanese soap operas on a big-screen TV. I'd like to see McCann-Erickson put *that* in one of those recruiting commercials.

"No worries, Señor. I got you covered. Sleep it off on the plane."

The plane in question is a jumbo jet, come to take us away to Saudi, to the war. We're waiting on the buses that will take us to that jumbo jet. Brawley brightens: "Oh, shit! Merry Christmas, Señor."

"It's Christmas. Well . . . season's beatings."

"Ain't that the fuckin' truth."

"Pretty good, huh? Saw that scribbled on a cocktail napkin last night. Stabbed to the top of the Christmas tree, or bush or whatever. Just a tarted-up stump, really. Even the Christmas trees on Okinawa look like whores. Sad."

"The best kind of sad, Señor."

A sweet smell sails in on the breeze. Evidently, the crematorium outside Gate 3 is open for business. Brawley squints into the dark. Spits. "Where the fuck are those fuckin' buses?"

Just then, one of those funny-looking Japanese minivans, a Nissan Vanette, I think, pulls up. And out of it come four white people, your basic middle-aged dudes and their ladies, civilians, waving pocket-size Bibles and baggies of cookies, like vendors hawking beer at a ball game. They're missionaries, come to lay blessings on us before we wreak the Lord's vengeance in the Gulf. The Bibles are the kind you'd see in a magazine, with a big-ass bullet hole torn through and some caption about how that Bible, *the armor of God worn over his heart,* saved their life. "God Bless America," and all that patriotic feculence. But it's those cookies I'm excited about. As a Marine, you're used to getting fucked. So you take your pleasures, however small, where you can get 'em.

"We're with Crusade for Christ, a Christian missionary group outside Gate 2 at Kadena, right in the middle of all those bars . . ."

It's the blonde. She's all business. "Nurse Ratched" from *One Flew over the Cuckoo's Nest* in an oversize "Just Say No!" T-shirt, dispensing the Word of God like bitter medicine. She hands us each a bag of cookies to make the medicine go down. Chocolate chip. Possibly homemade. Brawley immediately inhales his.

"Bible, Lieutenant?"

"No, thank you, ma'am. Be wasted on me."

"No Bible, no cookies, Marine."

She snatches the cookies from my hand and wanders over to Lance Corporal Gibbs, his sweaty brown face beaming a toothpaste-commercial smile. Fucker asks her to *pray* with him. Gibbs is the biggest kiss ass and thief in the battalion. When they're done, she gives Gibbs three bags of cookies and a goddamn hug. He smiles at me as if to say: *That's how it's done, Lieutenant.*

Fuckin' Gibbs. But he makes me laugh.

Four hours later we're still waiting for those buses. I doze on and off, my head on my helmet, like a pillow. I wake up groggy, neck stiff, as Black Santa weaves through hooting Marines on a comically small moped.

Brawley wheezes. Spits. Shuffles a deck of cards: "I'm a gamblin' fool, Señor. How 'bout a little blackjack? I'm feelin' lucky . . ."

"Staff Sergeant?"

Brawley squints up from his cards; Lance Corporal Colón, from Headquarters Company, stands over him, blocking the 120-watt Okinawa sun.

"The Pope needs to see you . . ."

The Pope was Chaplain Pope, our battalion chaplain, a Baptist minister actually, but some of the Marines began calling him "The Pope" and it stuck.

Brawley stares at Colón. "He say what about?"

"No, Staff Sergeant. He said to bring all your trash."

Brawley gathers his gear and his few personal belongings, mostly just a roll of Copenhagen and a couple of truck magazines from the PX, and stands, looking at me.

"I was gonna save this for when we hit the plane, but fuck it . . ."

Brawley walks to the back of a Humvee, the driver and A-driver asleep in front. He digs through piles of identical olive-green gear dumped into the back of the vehicle; a look of pleasure floods his Hoosier Irish face.

"Close your eyes."

"You're not gonna hit me, are you?"

Brawley wheezes. Spits. "I'm not gonna hit you, Señor. You're my favorite lieutenant. Just close your eyes."

I close my eyes.

"And keep 'em closed . . ."

When I open them, Brawley hands me one of the cardboard boxes the missionaries were carrying, filled with baggies of cookies. "Ol' Gibbs swiped 'em off them missionaries, sneaky little fucker. And I swiped 'em off Gibbs." He smiles. "Merry Christmas, Señor."

Brawley bear hugs me and humps off to see The Pope. It was the last time I ever saw him.

Exiled

Here's a little secret: the Marine Corps needs enemies. It lives for them. Whether it's banzai-charging Japanese, Chinese hordes, or boogeyman Vietcong—it doesn't matter. And when it can't find an enemy? *The Marine Corps eats its young.* And for Lieutenant Colonel "Mad Mike" Madigan, battalion commander, Lieutenant Francis Keane is perfect.

It all starts back in August, just before the first Persian Gulf War, on deployment to Okinawa, when one of Keane's "lance criminals," as Mad Mike calls them, punches out an NCO over a bar girl. *Alcohol related,* as the logbook duly notes. Keane—because he's a bleeding heart, a fool, or just a masochist—saves his ass from the brig. Mad Mike goes high and to the right. Because when the old man says "circle the wagons"—you circle the goddamn wagons.

As payback, Keane suffers every shit job and indignity, until finally exiled to the BOQ, the bachelor officers' quarters, and put in "hack," a kind of house arrest, for violating the Seventh General Order of the Sentry—to talk to no one except in the line of duty—while serving as

44

officer of the day. And so, into exile Keane goes, like some biblical mystic, alone and barefoot.

Word spreads. From his monk's cell in the BOQ, Keane receives a steady stream of enlisted Marines, of all races and ethnicities, bearing gifts of beef jerky, cans of beer, and soft-core pornography from the shelves of the PX. Even Honey, the offending bar girl, the face that launched a thousand fists, makes a tray of lumpia and chow-fun noodles. Keane becomes a folk hero.

Mad Mike's humiliations seem only to intensify Keane's fame. And it's the way Keane bears his wounds, bordering on insubordination, that makes Mad Mike absolutely lose his shit. Keane's resolve is geologic, like the limestone caves riddling the hills surrounding their Okinawan base, where doomed Japanese took cover from Marine fury during the war, to be blasted out by satchel charges and flamethrowers. Mad Mike is going to bunker buster the son of a bitch.

▲

That February, on the eve of the ground war in the Gulf, that most blessed of Marine events since the ruin of the Vietcong at Hue City, Mad Mike finally gets his chance, dispatching Keane and his Marines to a vacant grid co-ordinate, miles from the battalion now assembling along the Kuwaiti border, to load fifty-five-gallon drums of oil onto a five-ton truck. And with each drum weighing almost five hundred pounds, it's clearly a setup. They have no forklift. No special equipment. No tools other than misappropriated youth.

And, best of all, there will be no Combat Action Ribbon, that coveted bit of cloth, for Keane and his men—Mad Mike's personal "fuck you."

Now stripped to their T-shirts and soaked with sweat as they work, Keane's Marines shiver in the sharp air. They talk loudly as the February sun dissolves behind an oily veil. *It's cold, dawg!* They laugh, shrugging off the casual brutality of being Marines, their bosses referring to them as "bodies" instead of "men," the long absences from family. The comical pay. Yet they don't begrudge the Marine Corps their deal—not at all. It's far preferable to anonymous lives installing cable or drywall, invisible men from the American fringe, lives flaring hot and then going cold—for now, at least, they are *Marines*. And if that demands a ruined back or a nagging limp from loading oil drums in a far-off desert, well, then, so be it.

Keane lends his own back to the task just like anyone else. One more swingin' dick. Just another body.

Then something shifts in the air, almost imperceptibly. The Marines snap to, focusing like dogs catching scent of a threat, noses twitching, tails erect. In the distance: the sound of a groaning diesel engine.

Keane stands carefully, using the truck bumper for support, an old man at twenty-five, and goes forward to meet the still-unseen vehicle. Whatever, whoever it is—it isn't good.

The diesel rattles closer.

As the vehicle materializes in the pearly smoke, the Marines mass behind Keane instinctively. The Humvee's blacked-out headlights burn flatly in the sandy gloom, stopping abruptly, as if surprised to see Keane and his men. The engine cuts with a severe finality.

The passenger door bangs open, and Mad Mike tumbles out in a pale fury. Behind him, Corporal Lowe uncoils his long frame apologetically from the driver's seat. He cautiously surveys Keane's platoon, calculating the odds. Mad Mike is finished with the pleasantries, the possum playing, the eggshell walking. That shit is dead. Dead as dirt.

Mad Mike stands with hands on hips and squints, a straight-to-video Wyatt Earp before the gunfight at the OK Corral. And like the actors who've played the role before him, Mad Mike hopes his performance is convincing.

"Good afternoon, shitbirds." He spits tobacco into a plastic water bottle and smiles.

The Marines stare dumbly.

"Where's he hiding? *Lieutenant* Shitbird?"

Keane swallows hard, his throat stricken by fear as much as thirst. "Here, sir."

"What the hell was that? Sound off like you got some stones, Lieutenant."

"HERE, SIR!"

"Get over here."

Mad Mike stabs the air with a cocktail-weenie forefinger. "Right here, lad. Where I can see you."

Keane obeys.

Mad Mike is a Kodiak man; the tobacco packs his lower lip defiantly, his jaw set like a cartoon bulldog's. He stops. It's happening again—the nausea, all of it. Colored lights, like tiny explosions, a kaleidoscope of broken glass, jagged and sharp, sear his eyes. Mad Mike blinks back the pain. He hears them, the whispers, the little voices, seemingly mocking him. *If he could only understand what they were saying.*

It hurts, this mask. The headaches. The grinding. The twitching. But what's a little jaw distress, a migraine or concussion or whatever it is, when you're responsible for bearing the weight of two centuries of Marine Corps mythology?

His wintergreen and MRE coffee-sour breath blows hot and labored in Keane's face.

"What you got goin' here, Lieutenant?" he asks carefully, trying not to slur, the pain slowly subsiding. "I come to check up on you, and everybody's just hangin' out—think you're back on the beach at K-Bay? Aloha Friday?"

Keane stares, confused, his mind a blank.

"I asked you a question, Lieutenant. Come to attention when I'm speaking to you. I'm not Staff Sergeant Brawley," he manages a laugh, "your little beer-drinkin' buddy."

Keane stiffens. "It's just us out here, sir. We need a forklift . . ."

"Shut your suck, Lieutenant." Mad Mike spits into his water bottle again, chasing it with a hit off a Coke can he holds in his other hand.

"You know what pisses me off? *Excuses.* Especially from know-it-all lieutenants." He indicates the staring Marines with a sweep of his Coke can. "You think 'cause they buy you Courvoisier at Bosses Night they *love* you? 'Cause they play dominoes with you?" Mad Mike squeezes his head, as if threatening to come apart again. His hand shakes. But after a moment, he steadies, and smiles, as if to say: *Mad Mike don't go down for nobody.* "You think this is a popularity contest? *Lieutenant.*"

Mad Mike's words are sticky, with special emphasis placed on "Lieutenant," an accusation further reinforcing Keane's subshit status, just one more insubstantial goat turd in a desert full of insubstantial goat turds. Mad Mike tosses the Coke can, matter-of-factly unholsters the .45 strapped to his chest.

"You know what this is?"

Keane stares at the weapon. "It's a forty-five, sir."

"No shit. You know what else this is? My *authority.* Says I can do whatever the fuck I want."

Mad Mike chambers a round. "You understand who's runnin' the show here, right?" He raises the pistol above his head. It *bangs*—three times—like a judge's gavel, the spent brass clinking lonely onto the sand.

"I am." He points the pistol accusingly at Keane. "I find you guilty of being a disloyal fuck. Gimme your bars and get in the vehicle, Lieutenant—*former* Lieutenant. I am relieving you of command."

Keane clears his throat. Considers his words. "Sir? My father always said: you point a weapon at a man, you better be ready to kill him."

Mad Mike leans into Keane, his attention feral, almost carnal—under different circumstances, a prelude to a kiss possibly. But there will be no kiss. Warily, Keane waits for the punch line, as Mad Mike lets out a long, slow belch—turning to smile at Corporal Lowe, then back at Keane.

The tang of booze lingers stubbornly in the slurry of Mad Mike's breath: Wild Turkey and warm Coke—the specialty of the house, courtesy, no doubt, of the free-market capitalists running the AT&T tent back at Manifa.

"That is what I think of you—and your old man." Mad Mike attempts to reholster his pistol. After several tries, he gives up. The pistol becomes a burden, more deadweight to bear.

Keane dares a look at Mad Mike, a cut shorter, twenty years older, and a thousand beers heavier. Oddly, perhaps, given his immediate peril, Francis registers Mad Mike's cheeks—pitted, like pricks from an ice pick, leftovers from an unimaginable adolescence, burning pink now from booze, almost like blush. Odder still, their color reminds Keane of the bougainvillea growing in Norma's yard, his girlfriend back in Honolulu—and her ability to extract suffering from him, like venom sucked from a snakebite. Her hands, the hands of an artist, possess a kind of magic, to create, to cure, to heal. And in that moment, Keane realizes that he hasn't been touched by Norma—or any human—in more than a year.

And deep within Mad Mike, a seed takes root—of failure. Of *defeat*. Not in the mundane realm of "winners and losers"—all just football scores really, ultimately meaningless—but a personal failing, and the realization this failing was a chain, thousands of years long, that bound him, made him a prisoner, and that he willingly pledged himself to this chain, out of fear, like a fatal flaw.

Yet, for Mad Mike, there was only one way out—and that was forward.

"Give me your bars and get in the back of the vehicle, Lieutenant. Now."

Surely, this order is rooted in an ingrained faith in the established order of things, the trappings of a rational society, a place where citizens stop at stop signs, say "Please" and "Thank you," and all Marines, well trained, respect small pieces of metal on an officer's collar, denoting status and rank. It's also a place where personal mythologies, when alchemized with tribal beliefs, transform fallible human beings, the most common of men, into demigods and lords to be feared—the heroes of sports, war, and politics—the Mad Mikes, slave princes of conquest, all.

This is no longer that place.

Keane remains silent. He's felt it too, this shift. This lifting of the veil. And despite his still considerable fear, he smiles, with directness and simplicity—acknowledging, for a brief moment, their shared intimacy. Mad Mike waves the pistol impatiently, as if swatting an annoying bug.

"Let's go, Lieutenant."

And even as he does it, it feels otherworldly, unbelievable—as if someone else, someone much braver and reckless, is doing it. Keane, dizzy with fear, slaps the forty-five from Mad Mike's hand, ejecting the round from the chamber and the magazine from the grip. He launches the magazine into the wind, watching in disbelief as it sails off.

Mad Mike's right eye twitches—just barely. It might just be TMJ, the migraine aftershocks, whatever, but it's done. Irretrievable. Still in disbelief, Keane presents the weapon to Mad Mike, almost whispering: "Muzzle discipline, sir."

Even as it plays out in front of them, no one will remember what happened, or if indeed it did happen, so unthinkable the total collapse of two hundred years of dogma, an unimaginable heresy.

Some things are best forgotten.

There is no return; Mad Mike at least understands that. He steps back from Keane, hawks a defiant stream of Kodiak into the dirt, and announces into the darkening air: "I don't have time to hold your hand, Lieutenant. I got a war to win. A nation to liberate. Bad guys to punish. Get that vehicle back to battalion. ASAP."

Mad Mike wheels on his boot and beelines for the Humvee, barking at Lowe: "Saddle up!" Lowe refolds his body back into the cramped vehicle as Mad Mike stares straight ahead and the Humvee jars awake, does a slow U-turn, and disappears into the orange-rind twilight, back to the war and the glory.

Keane watches the Humvee melt away, its uncertain diesel growing fainter until, finally, all is silent again. He turns to his Marines, and they regard one another as from opposite shores, across a great gulf, in terms of rank, certainly, but also in terms of race and even class. But they understand something about each other—indefinable, something that cannot be put into mere words or even spoken aloud. Something ancient.

They will live within one another, always.

War is inevitable, without end. You choose your sides. There are no guarantees. There will always be another Mad Mike. And like the Marine Corps itself, Mad Mike is as immortal as the snow-globed desert dusk now surrounding them.

So while the night wind snakes across the dusty floor, Keane eyeballs the oil drums, just dark shapes now, and spits.

The Mail Thief

Some would have called Lance Corporal Colón a thief. Technically, Colón stole mail, which of course is a federal crime (five years in federal prison and up to $250,000 in fines). I say "technically" because Colón always returned whatever he stole to the proper addressee. Who, as far as I could tell, was only me.

You see, Colón was our battalion "mailman." His MOS, or "military occupational specialty," was admin clerk, which is as exciting as it sounds—keeping records, typing, and other clerical shit—but Colón also delivered mail when we were deployed, as we were, to the Persian Gulf. Everyone had one or two jobs in addition to their regular job, and Colón was lucky in a way; he could've been a "SAC-A," or "substance-abuse control assistant," in charge of the piss bottles during drug tests, also known as "meat gazer." But that was Montague's collateral duty. Colón was only a mailman.

Colón was Puerto Rican, or Dominican maybe. From the South Bronx, I think. The kind of place that shows up on the news only after something bad happened. I liked Colón. He wasn't like the other young Marines. He was thoughtful. Curious. Kind of lost. Which explains how he ended up in the Marines. Kind of like me, maybe.

Most mornings, I'd come out of a bunker where I'd spent the night, hungover by life, to be greeted by a smiling Colón, an armful of mail for me from home. There'd be stuff from my girlfriend, Norma, a jewelry designer, back in Hawaii; she loved putting together care packages for me and my Marines: Hawaii junk food, like dried cuttlefish, rock-salt plum, saimin noodles, and whatever subversive or pornographic art she'd make. She'd identify each Marine by name on the package; they loved that. My mom sent snickerdoodles, chalk-dry sugar cookies that I'd liked for ten minutes in the second grade, that we'd feed to the kangaroo rats sharing our bunkers. And from my dad, a Marine pilot in Vietnam, postcards with inspirational sayings dashed off in a large loopy hand, almost feminine, signed with a spirited *Semper Fi, Marine!* There'd always be plenty of "To Any Marine" letters as well, from elementary schools across the country, with crayoned epics of Iraqi soldiers engulfed in flames, and the Polaroids from anonymous bikini and lingerie patriots doing their part to lift our morale.

And then there were the magazines, a lifeline to a world outside the Marines, where people thought big thoughts, did big things, and had big times in places like London, New York, and Los Angeles. So I subscribed to the *LA Weekly*, the *Village Voice, Paper, Esquire*, the *New Yorker*—all the usual suspects, devoured in a multitude of sandy holes pockmarking the Saudi desert like adolescent acne. I was cuckoo for magazines.

But after a while, I noticed my magazines would arrive smudgy and pawed, with covers missing and pages torn out, especially pictures of supermodels or actresses. This was distressing. I mean, I *needed* a picture of Winona Ryder rolling those big brown eyes for my bunker wall. She helped keep me sane.

Yet it was wartime and the mail was coming from far away, so I didn't think too much of it at first. *C'est la guerre!* Right? But the real shock came when I realized that Norma's care packages had been pilfered—*ratfucked*, as we'd say in the Marines.

Again, whatever. Weird shit happens. But one day I get a letter from Norma. She asked if I liked the book she'd sent: *Alien Sex*, an anthology of science fiction pornography. Sex with robots. Tentacles. That kinda thing. That absolutely got my attention. So I hitched a ride down to Manifa, the division bivouac, maybe two hours south, to ask the admin bubbas what was up with the mail. I got there and Manifa was deserted.

So nobody expected me when I appear in the admin hooch. As my eyes adjusted to the dark, I discovered a gagglefuck of admin clerks jockeying around a field desk. Their heads snapped toward the door at the sudden flood of light, scurrying like silverfish when they realized I was an officer. And there's Colón, hunched over my *Alien Sex*, the Saudi sunlight spotlighting him like a goddamn movie.

"What the fuck, Colón?"

Colón looked up casually from my *Alien Sex*. A bloody Kleenex dangled from his nostril.

"Hey, sir . . ."

"Don't 'Hey, sir' me. What're you doing with my mail?"

"Sir, I'm just reading it, sir . . . I'm gonna return it, sir . . ."

He couldn't say "sir" enough times. As if this alone would placate me. The admin clerks, absorbed anew in their ledgers, logbooks, and personnel files, like a mime troupe parodying "work," had their collective third eyes trained on me and Colón, ready to hit the deck if necessary.

"Let's go. Outside."

Colón dutifully followed, a dog being led to his kennel. He handed me the book.

"Here, sir."

"Get the Kleenex outta your nose, please." Colón obeyed.

"Let's talk a walk, lad."

As we walked through the bivouac, I tried to play the role of "angry alpha dog," but it was pretty much impossible. First off, the way Colón looked. I mean, he's built like some cartoon character, a spider maybe, with these long arms and legs and this short body; fucker was all of five-foot-three. And he had an almost perfectly round head, geometrically speaking, a sphere. It's big too, and fuzzy like a cartoon. *All* out of proportion. I think he cuts his own hair too. And he had a pair of what we call "BCGs," or "birth-control glasses"—Marine-issue glasses so fucking ugly you'd never get laid wearing them, big brown-orange squares that morphed Colón's eyes into one giant worried Cyclopean eye. And he's got these troubled brows, like two caterpillars boxing, and a mustache, I guess you'd call it. The finishing touch is this .45-caliber pistol, an engorged piece of metal, an obscenity drooping from his right hip like Deputy Dawg. It's so heavy that Colón actually limps when he walks. He's not even authorized to carry a .45. But again, for all these reasons, and more, I find it impossible to be angry with this kid. Because that's what he is, really, a kid. Nineteen or twenty at the oldest.

"Colón," I sigh.

He turns his spheroid head to me, brows sparring nervously. "Sir."

"Seriously. What the fuck? Mail theft is a federal crime."

"Yes, sir."

He says this as if resigned to his fate. He'll swallow poison; he'll drown himself in the Gulf—as I demand.

"Why?"

His hands go wide in mute frustration, fingers spread, as if to emphasize their emptiness, their inability to thieve. Finally, Colón looks up at me with his colossal eye.

"You've got interesting mail, sir."

I laugh. "What does that mean?"

Blood trickles from his nose. "My nose is bleeding, sir."

"I see that." I remove the olive-green T-shirt that I'm using as a scarf from around my neck, hand it to Colón.

"Thank you, sir. It's dry. The desert, I mean. I get nosebleeds when it's dry."

He tilts his head back and presses the filthy shirt to his nose. The nosebleed has seemingly loosened something in Colón. I hear his voice, muffled now, from beneath my shirt:

"I mean, most stuff to read here is like Victoria's Secret catalogs and *Leatherneck* and *Word Up!* Mouth-breather stuff. I've got nothing to read, sir."

I let this sink in. I'm a reader. Books were very important growing up. I just assumed everyone was the same. The printed word excited me, filled me with possibility. As long as I had a book, I was okay. At that very moment, I had a well-worn copy of *A Tree Grows in Brooklyn* tucked into my flak jacket. The idea that Colón had nothing to read was oddly affecting. I couldn't conceive of such a situation.

"What about your folks? Have them send you some books or something."

Colón removes my shirt from his nose and looks at me as if I've said the dumbest thing imaginable.

"Okay . . . maybe not. How about the Commandant's Reading List? There's gotta be something from that list floating around the battalion."

The commandant, who's like the pope of the Marines, initiated an official "reading list" a few years back. Surprising—but the Marines, paradoxically maybe, like to think of themselves as a marriage of violence and scholarship.

"I don't want to read books about Marines, sir." I don't blame him.

"Yeah, but isn't there some sci-fi on that list? *Starship Troopers*? That's a classic. You like sci-fi." I wave *Alien Sex* at him.

"I like the *New Yorker*, sir. 'Shouts and Murmurs.' The 'Fiction.'"

"So get a subscription."

"I make $878.10 a month, sir. I got an allotment for my mom and sister. Some parking tickets I'm still paying off." We look at each other.

"You're a mess, aren't you?"

"Yes, sir."

Now it's my turn to be silent. We keep walking, past the shitters, past a burning trash pit, past a makeshift boxing ring, made up of howling Marines, calling for blood as two face off, wearing work gloves instead of boxing gloves. Colón ignores all this, this planet of men, walking with hands clasped behind his back, like an old man out for a walk, a Puerto Rican Alvy Singer from a reimagined *Annie Hall*. We come to the Baskin-Robbins trailer. Colón turns to me:

"Are you going to put me up on charges, sir?"

"Fuck no." His brows relax.

"Thank you, sir. I really appreciate it."

"No more 'borrowing' mail, okay?"

"No more, sir. I'm done."

"Good."

I look at Colón, clap my hands twice: "That's it. Fort Pitt." Colón is confused.

"Sir?"

"Oh. That's just something my dad would do when something was finished. It's from a beer commercial. Fort Pitt beer. 'That's it. Fort Pitt.'" I catch the scent of something sweet. The smell of ice cream mixes with burning garbage and whatever else is on fire.

"You want a cone?"

Colón answers carefully, as if it might be a trick question: "Sure, sir . . ."

We sit atop a pile of sandbags, eating our ice cream.

"How's the book?"

"Sir?"

"Alien Sex."

"Oh." Colón holds back, hedges his bets: "It's good."

"Good? That's a terrible word."

"Yessir. There's a story about a scientist, who's married, but falls in love with an orangutan he's doing experiments on." He quickly adds: "A female one."

"Interesting."

"Sir?"

"Yes, Colón?"

"This is yours too."

Colón hands me a cassette, a mixtape from Norma. *Fuck Music* written on it in ballpoint pen.

"Thank you, Colón."

"I'm sorry, sir."

From my flak jacket, I hand Colón A *Tree Grows in Brooklyn.* "Read this. It's good. She's a New York kid like you. Loves books."

Colón has this stunned look on his face. I'm not sure anyone's ever given him a present before. I scribble inside the cover: *To LCPL Colón: A smart guy. A good Marine. Keep reading! Semper Fi! 1st Lieutenant Francis Keane, Manifa, Saudi Arabia, 1991.*

Norma started sending Colón books soon after: *Lolita, Tropic of Cancer,* J. G. Ballard's *Crash.* Classic literature masquerading as pornography, as was her specialty.

I got him a subscription to the *New Yorker* and the *Village Voice*. What the hell, right? I didn't have a family, no kids yet. I'd just spend the money on beer anyway. He was thrilled. We kind of "adopted" Colón in a way, at least temporarily. When he bitched about how bad Saudi hamburgers were, I took him to get shawarma. Pita bread. Hummus. When we got back to Hawaii, Norma and I took Colón out for Japanese food—sushi, sashimi, ramen noodles, you name it. He loved it.

Then one day, I discovered that my Doc Marten shoes were missing from my car, parked on base. (I never locked my doors.) I was pissed at first, but it's like they say—"the only thing you can trust a Marine with is your life." About a week later, I'm at the PX, and who did I cross paths with? Colón. And he was wearing my goddamn Doc Martens. (We're both a 10.5 D apparently.) Let's just say we were both surprised to see each other. I let him know that I knew, but I didn't do anything about it. I needed a new pair anyway.

Later, when I transferred to Headquarters Marine Corps in Arlington, Virginia, Colón would call me from the pay phone outside the Enlisted Club at Camp Hansen, in Okinawa. He'd be drunk of course, bitching about the battalion and "all the mouth breathers." I'd give him a pep talk, encourage him to keep reading, keep learning. This, remember, is from the guy who couldn't afford a subscription to the *New Yorker*. I don't even want to imagine how much those calls cost. After a while, Colón stopped calling.

Why put up with Colón's shit, you ask? The simple answer is that I'm a "bleeding heart," a sucker. But that's hard to accept. Marines are supposed to be "tough." But the official answer, the one I give myself in defense of being that sucker, is that I felt I had a responsibility to return my Marines better human beings than I found them, more open to the possibility of the world. At the very least, I wanted their eyes to be open. To be curious. That was my "collateral duty." But that's all bullshit obviously—pretty words to soothe my Irish Catholic guilt that I was somehow less than a "real" Marine because I'd indulged Colón, that I'd failed somehow.

But if I'm being honest, there's another part of me that missed Colón's attention. His adoration, I suppose you'd call it. It's embarrassing to admit, but it was nice having someone look up to you, thinking you're brilliant and that your thoughts were worth listening to, that not only your mail but even your shoes were worth stealing.

Gas

You want to see a Marine freak out? Tell him he's got ten seconds to "don and clear" his gas mask because there's a cloud of nerve gas coming his way.

I stood in a pit, the entranceway to our bunker, brushing my teeth, thinking of nothing. Just across the border in Kuwait, burning oil wells pulsed against a black sky. It was late January 1991, outside Khafji, Saudi Arabia. *Bumfucknowhere*, as my Marines might say. From hidden speakers, warning voices broke open the night, strangely detached, as if announcing departing flights at an airport.

"*Gas. Gas. Gas. Mopp 4. Mopp 4. This is not a drill . . .*"

Ghost sirens, like the wailing of lost children, called out from the desert.

Fuck.

Mopp gear was what you wore in case of a chemical or biological attack—a bulky charcoal-lined suit, with hood, gloves, rubber boot covers, and a gas mask, Munch's *Scream*, but without luxury of a mouth, the stuff of dread. Toothpaste dribbling from my chin, I watched my Marines tumble out of the bunker, half-asleep and cursing, struggling into their Mopp gear. Sergeant Travis asked where I wanted the machine guns, but my mind remained a guilty blank. As lieutenant, the "boss man"— I'm supposed to know such things.

Staff Sergeant Brawley, lip packed with Copenhagen, jogged toward me from somewhere in the dark, a "victory lap" of sorts, all swagger and cool, as if he'd just knocked out his opponent in the first round of the Golden Gloves and was headed for a hot shower.

"Hola, Señor . . ."

Señor: Brawley's nickname for me. He called me that when we were drinking beer. I hadn't had a beer in months.

"Hola." The word caught, as if too big for my throat. Brawley's pale eyes lit up the dark.

"Me and ol' Gibbs was playin' bones, down in Ops. Recon reported a shit ton of tanks crossin' the border, up in Khafji." He pointed to an orange blur on the horizon, where Khafji apparently lay, burning. "A whole Iraqi armor division. Saudis bolted, so it's wide open; they're just cruisin' on down, like it's the Paddy's Day parade in Fort Wayne." Brawley worked his dip. "Looks like we're earnin' our pay tonight, Señor."

Most people, myself included, would have considered this to be very bad news, but Brawley just laughed. Maybe he was different from me—from the rest of us, his Hoosier Irish veins full of something more.

Lying on the berm, I watched the sky in front of me burn white with tracers and silent explosions, like heat lightning from the beginning of the world, when all was darkness and void. I heard my breathing, labored and loud in the mask, threatening to betray me. My heart jackrabbited against my ribs, eager to run, looking for an exit, but with nowhere to go. I couldn't see. The small pair of prescription glasses that fitted into the mask were thousands of miles away, somewhere in Okinawa. My pistol was filthy too, a hanging offense—the slide full of demon sand.

As I'd removed the pistol from the holster, I thought about my father, a Marine pilot in Vietnam. Flew 307 missions. Won a chestful of medals—the whole deal. He even carried a Smith and Wesson *Victory*—that's the actual name, it's a six-shooter—like some spaghetti-western cowboy ready for his wide-screen shoot-out.

My pistol, in comparison, seemed Mickey Mouse, a toy or prop, with all the gravity of a child going *bang-bang* with his finger. Only officers carry pistols, so they're special, symbols more than anything, of authority—like a scepter or a badge, a judge's gavel, even. My father once told me of how he shot a Marine in the foot for disobeying an order. Probably bullshit, but it didn't matter. Some part of me still believed my pistol possessed actual magic, magic that would transfer to me—transform me—if I held it long enough.

Marines flickered in and out of shadow as they ran crouched along the berm, underneath the stony light of gently hanging flares, eyeing me, as if expecting some kind of answer, a solution.

I squeezed my pistol until my hand ached.

A rocket—then a flash. The ground shot upward. Brawley stumbled and fell the last few yards, like a disciple bowing in prayer, landing heavily across my back. He placed his mask against mine, pulling me close, his voice soothing above the roar.

"Ain't this some shit." I could hear his smile. He was clearly having the time of his life. "You good, Señor?"

I stared at him through our masks, his blue eyes focused and calm, tempted to spill my guts—but I held back. Truth was, I didn't need to say anything. Brawley knew. And that was okay.

He squeezed me tight, his Golden Gloves boxer's arm across my back, big and beautiful and reassuring, and like that, as if it was Brawley's arm that contained the real magic, it was over. With the help of some unseen Cobra helicopters, all those tanks became just more burning things on the horizon.

Over cold MREs at breakfast, Lance Corporal Gibbs gleefully announced: "Hey, Lieutenant, sir! I saw you last night."

"That was *you*? You stalking me, Lance Corporal?" I said, knowing Gibbs was gonna dump on me. It was part of our routine.

"Yes, indeed, I did. And you weren't smilin'. No sir." Everyone laughed. Even me. Because it was true. I wanted no part of this. No part of the con.

Shortly after we got back, my father died, prostate cancer—Agent Orange. His Smith and Wesson Victory just rusty metal now, unable to save him. Brawley's gone too, throat cancer—all that dip. Me? I've got sleep apnea.

Ulcerative colitis. Tinnitus. The VA sends me a check every month, "beer money" mostly. I guess only the Marine Corps is immortal.

But for now? I'm alive. And I'm not unhappy about that.

The Trigger Pullers

Mad Mike wiped out a herd of camels the very first night. Lieutenant Keane, on duty in the Ops Center with Gunner McKee, swore it was an Iraqi armor unit. But in the darkness just before dawn, he couldn't be 100 percent sure. So Keane woke Mad Mike, our battalion commander—and let him make the call. Mad Mike harbored no such doubts—he was not an indecisive man.

"Have TOWs take 'em out," Mad Mike growled.

TOWs were antitank missiles. Mad Mike wasn't going to miss out on the first kill of the war because Lieutenant Keane couldn't tell the difference between a Soviet-made self-propelled gun and a goddamn camel.

So TOWs took 'em out.

That's the kind of war it was. We killed camels.

That's not to say we weren't bloody too, morally, I mean, a known constant in the calculus leading to shitloads of dead Iraqis—while Americans back home bitched about the price of gas. Even in the supposed free-for-all known as "the ground war," we were spectators, watching as tanks, aircraft, and artillery did the actual slaughter—"processing," we cynically called it, as if simply stuffing sausage through some factory.

What followed was a Marine Corps–specific hell—a kind of penance for our bystander status during the war—mindless inspections, endless PT, and "hip-pocket" classes on balancing your checkbook or grenade-launcher maintenance. For one brief moment we were liberators, freeing the nation of Kuwait from their Iraqi oppressors, and the next it was *Trim that mustache, Lance Corporal.* The comedown was bad, worse than a hundred Camp Hansen Bosses Night hangovers. Once the rah-rah letters from the schoolkids stopped coming and the "thank-you" cookouts hosted by grateful oil companies dished their last hot dogs, I slipped into an unshakable funk.

One night, back at the division bivouac at Manifa, I watched as some tough-luck PFC doused shitters with diesel fuel in preparation for burning. The PFC went about his task soberly, like an undertaker preparing for a viewing. Bored Marines gathered, eating ice cream cones from the nearby Baskin-Robbins trailer. Now, with an audience, the PFC injected a bit of ceremony into his mundane task, showering not only the shit in the fifty-five-gallon drums with diesel, but the entire plywood structure as well. One of the Marines flicked a burning cigarette, and the soaked shitter went up with a *whoosh.* The flames attracted more Marines. They brought scraps of wood, MRE boxes, and ammo crates—anything that would burn—and tossed them into the fire. One Marine, who'd assumed the role of a half-assed ringmaster, broke open a chemlight and smeared his face with the glowing pink goo, like war paint. He stripped down to his boots, tossed his uniform onto the pyre and pissed on the inferno, his urine illuminated by the flames, orange and bright, like tracer rounds, while his skinny body shone blue and cold, the color of moonlight. But it was just a distraction, something to do until we went home, like the "Rowdy in Saudi" fights, hundreds of us, in helmets and flak jackets, basically beating the shit out of each other for fun in the middle of the desert, or calling Colonel Madigan, our battalion commander, "Camel Killer" be-hind his back—instead of "Mad Mike"—the nickname he'd given himself, something he'd seen in a movie. The party officially shit the bed when someone tossed an M16 magazine into the fire, Gunny Gittens scolding us in his Barbadian lilt, which always sounded like he was singing. As we scattered, howling with laughter, the rounds cooking off in the flames, I couldn't help but feel our four-day victory might well be the marquee event of our lives, the peak summited, everything following just a long, slow slide.

So the next day, when Vargas, a Weapons Company machine gunner of dangerous proportions, rolled up in a Humvee looking for help surveying gear down at the port, I jumped in, eager to get outta Dodge, even if it was only down to Jubail.

Vargas only looked ominous. Silent as the empty roads carved into the sandy scrub of his hometown of Eagle Pass, Texas, Vargas was built like one of the bulls on his family's ranch. Dude was *made* for war, made for slinging .50-cal machine guns over recruiting-poster shoulders with a mighty ease. I'd be tempted to say that I was the brains of our friendship and Vargas the brawn, but that wouldn't be accurate. In addition to being built like a Mexican minotaur, Vargas graduated second in his class at Eagle Pass. He even had a rodeo scholarship to Texas A&M, but like his old man, Vargas joined the Marines. My skinny Cajun ass barely graduated. It was the Marines or McDonald's for Kenny Fontenot.

We cruised the port, cranking Metallica's . . . *And Justice for All* on a boom box wedged between the seats, rocking out like we were anywhere but Saudi, regular teenagers, headed to the Sonic after the game for chili-cheese tots and seven minutes in heaven. Battalion rumor control had been buzzing about Danish nurses down at Jubail who didn't have cots—nurses who, owing to their lax Danish morality, would supposedly fuck you to get one. So it became our mission to liberate cots from one of the warehouses down there and introduce our audacious selves to these sleep-deprived Danes. For an hour or two, I almost felt good.

We spent the morning creeping through the maze of loading docks and supply dumps on the hunt for these cots. Yet by noon, we'd found only two and a half cases of warm Fanta orange soda, stolen from some mess hall. We couldn't find a cot to save our ass.

As Vargas drove, his bulk low in the seat like some MTV gangster rapper, eyes barely over the steering wheel, we got into it about the nurses, whether they were one of those "too good to be true" rumors Marines live for. Was Denmark even one of the countries in the coalition? You have to understand, the United States Marine Corps runs on rumor. Mostly, these are of the "something bad is gonna happen" variety, because expecting bad shit to happen is part of the DNA of being a Marine. To balance it out, you've got the "wishful thinking" rumors, like with the nurses, or my favorite, that TV's Mister Rogers was a Marine sniper in Korea who'd racked up a record number of confirmed kills and wore those cardigans only to hide an arm full of "Born to Kill" tattoos.

We popped a couple of Fantas and straggled north, Vargas messing with the .45 that rode low on his thigh, a parting gift from his father who'd carried it during the siege of Khe Sanh in Vietnam. How cool is that? All my old man ever gave me was a thousand dollars in Camel Cash for Christmas one year. Vargas proudly told anyone who'd listen that Old Man Vargas was a warrior—that he'd won the Navy Cross during the famous Hill Fights of '67. So that .45 was more than just a simple gift; it was Vargas's *legacy*—a psychic part of him, inseparable from who he was, like being a Texan or his family name. That pistol became a kind of good-luck charm for Vargas, better than a rabbit's foot because you made your own magic with a .45.

We ran up the Coast Highway, the road rigidly defining our world, a narrow strip of sand running from the blacktop east to the oily Gulf. With the exception of the ground war, when we went west to join up with the division at al-Qarrah, we never ventured west of the road. There was no reason—nothing existed west of the highway, except goats, camels, and more sand. The highway itself was a bizarre parade of luxury and military vehicles. Humvees, five-ton trucks, and LAVs—light armored vehicles with 25mm chain guns and stenciled monster-truck names like "Gravedigger," "Fat Bastard," and "Doom Wagon" mixed with cars we'd seen only in music videos or movies: Benzos and Rolls, the occasional Caddy, their expensive colors startling against the sober tan of the military vehicles and brown Saudi desert, like strippers at an Amish funeral.

The Saudis were insane drivers. We discovered new crashes daily, head-on collisions so horrific as to actually make us question our own mortality. To voice such fears would have been unthinkable, though, sacrilegious even, so we expressed regret only at the destruction of such beautiful machines and the bonkers waste of money.

And, as mysteriously as they'd appear, the wrecks would vanish, leaving us to question whether we'd actually seen anything or if it was some kind of a mirage, like an oasis appearing to Popeye in an old cartoon, lost on his way to fight Ali Baba and his forty thieves. We'd sometimes stop to get a better look, admiring the craftsmanship of catastrophe like customers in some nightmare car showroom, feeling a perverse thrill at seeing something so expensive, so perfect, so wasted.

The cars were always empty, except for the few things they'd left behind: a woman's shoe, Arab music CDs, maybe a tube of lipstick. Mundane shit. In Saudi, death was everywhere. We just couldn't always see it.

And unlike the movies or TV, the way people died in Saudi was somehow shameful—Marines accidentally shot each other, got run over by trucks, and blew themselves up with their own grenades, the wreckage of thousands of teenagers with more testosterone than good sense let loose in the desert. "Shit happens," as the bumper sticker on my dad's truck says.

Back in February, at al-Qarrah, before the ground war kicked off, we hunkered at the berm, waiting to go north. The B-52s whined overhead in the dark, so low you could smell jet fuel burning; we heard the smothered thumps, felt the ground shake. And on the horizon, a distant inferno raged, red and bloated. It shimmered silently, up from the desert floor, like heat lightning in the predawn gloom. But we only watched it, safe—like the audience on some TV talk show, where Death hides behind a curtain, the surprise guest waiting for his cue.

But that was then.

On our way north we discovered an abandoned supply dump, just off the highway, a gumbo of ammo and canned spaghetti, still on pallets, the spaghetti wrapped in plastic with "Courtesy of the Mishawaka Rotary Club" stamped on the side. I leaped from pallet to pallet, with .50-cal ammo crisscrossing my chest like Frito Bandito, taking pictures of each other with the disposable camera my mom sent me.

Vargas stopped in the middle of all that spaghetti— America, *land of plenty!*—panting and out of breath, uncertainty on his normally certain face. He clutched at his holster, that big pistol heavy now on his thigh, a reminder of his spectator status in the Big Event of his life. The fact that Vargas hadn't fired his weapon, hadn't even *unholstered* it during the four-day ground war, hounded him, demanded his attention.

How would he explain this to his old man?

Vargas turned slowly, taking in the seemingly endless pallets surrounding him and fired all eight rounds of his .45 in a deafening fury, watching as spaghetti bled silently into the dirt.

▲

Cordite hung heavy in the dank cab of the Humvee, the metallic sting fusing with the sour sweat of our bodies, creating a bitter funk. Vargas was silent, his eyes dull and hard, like granite chips, as he drove, fixed on the shadowy road. Behind us, the sun burned low. Vargas drove fast, as if trying to outrun the darkness.

The March sky filled with stars, sparkling severe and cold. Metallica ground wearily on the boom box. The Humvee's dashboard, stark and spare, glowed dimly as we plunged into darkness, our headlights still in blackout mode, the big diesel engine lulling us into a half-sleep. As we neared a place we called "the Chicken Ranch," close to the cutoff for Manifa Bay Road, our headlights swept past another wreck. We startled awake, slowing to take in the damage—some kind of truck this time. But instead of continuing to the Marine checkpoint a couple miles down the road, Vargas pulled the Humvee over and stared off into the darkness, his big fists working the steering wheel, the idling engine the only sound. To intrude on his thoughts seemed dangerous. Vargas continued staring ahead, his face impassive. When I did speak, my voice was sharper than I'd intended.

"*Vargas.*"

His name hung in the air, like a bullet, midflight. I waited, almost hiding, afraid of his reaction, but to my surprise, his face softened, as if he'd solved a riddle.

"That truck, like one of the trucks the Mexicans use to work our ranch. That's a workingman's truck."

Vargas nodded, as if answering himself, threw the Humvee into gear, did a wide U-turn, and headed back to the wreck. I closed my eyes, escaping to the refuge of an old girlfriend smiling, the gap between her teeth still front and center, cocksure and wrong, before she got it fixed, removing her sweater over her head. But that only lasted so long.

A '70s Toyota truck took shape in the murky head-lights, one of those beaters Bedouin goat herders drove, where you got in from the passenger's side because the driver's door was held shut with a coat hanger. The truck was flipped onto its back, the front buried into the dirt, red and bent like a clown's nose, the cab crushed to half normal size. Vargas pointed the Humvee at the wreck. The headlights made the truck seem redder than it actually was, against the blackness of the desert night.

Vargas unlatched the Humvee's soft door and stepped out. Cool night air flooded the cab, sobering me. Reluctantly, I grabbed my rifle and closed behind Vargas, somehow more nervous than I'd been during the actual war. Our boots softly crunched desert grit as we approached the wreck, the Toyota's engine ticking sharply. The breeze smelled faintly of gasoline, carrying with it Metallica's "One" from the Humvee, as well as the briny tang of the Gulf, not more than a mile away. The decaying bite of the salt air was oddly comforting, memories, I guess, of little-kid trips to Holly Beach, the "Cajun Riviera," as my old man called it. A rare good memory.

Just outside the shattered cab, we discovered a pair of night-vision goggles, US military issue. Vargas crouched, his .45 trained on the truck cab with the same intensity as if hunting coyotes back home. I circled back instinctually, checking behind the vehicle, where I discovered four black plastic jerry cans, scattered and crushed in the dirt, gushing diesel in rhythmic thumps like a severed artery. Vargas called to me from the cab.

I hurried back, to find Vargas in perfect kneeling position, his .45 trained where the driver's window used to be.

He jerked his pistol toward the cab.

Vargas spit a wad of Skoal onto the ground for emphasis, wiping his mouth on his sleeve. I dropped to my belly for a better look. Buried among empty water bottles, food trash, and what looked like some kind of camera were two feet—one wearing a gold men's dress shoe, mesh wing tip, the kind you might wear to senior prom if you were Michael Jackson. The other foot was bare and calloused—no sock, nothing—the errant gold shoe lying on what was the roof of the cab. With the truck crushed on top of him and just his fancy feet sticking out, the poor fucker looked like the Wicked Witch of the West after Dorothy's house landed on her. Vargas tapped my boot—*let's go.*

We rounded the nose of the hissing truck, wary of who might be attached to those gold shoes, because if my nineteen years on this planet had taught me anything, it's that the world was an unpredictable and dangerous place, filled with men who court confusion, using it almost like bait. I squeezed the barrel of my rifle tighter.

As we stepped forward, we could just make out the form of a large man, well fed, and thus eliminating the possibility of his being Bedouin, who were famously scrawny. He lay on his side, illuminated just enough by the watery Humvee lights coming through the cab to tell he was what we called a "Haji"—an Arab male—wearing one of those "man dresses." He was alone—and very dead as far as I could tell. I leaned in for a closer look. His face, round and ripe, was freshly shaven except for a clipped mustache, almost military in its restraint, smelling faintly of cologne, a piney woodland scent out of place in the ruined Saudi desert. His right arm was trapped beneath his heavy body, the other arm was outstretched, as if reaching for something. His paw-like hand was soft and unblemished by labor. An expensive watch, gaudy and gold like his shoes, bound his thick wrist like a cuff. A broad wedding band, simple in contrast, was buried in the flesh of his ring finger. For some reason, that ring got me—this guy had a wife somewhere, kids maybe, who didn't know he was lying by the side of the road with two Marines poking at him like a flattened possum.

Beyond his hand, just out of reach, lay a satellite phone. At this, I was ready to get the hell out and let Lieutenant Keane take over the mystery. He's an officer. Let *him* figure it out. Instead, Vargas turned and nodded toward the truck.

"You're skinnier than me. Take a look in the cab."

Fuck.

Grudgingly, I returned to the driver's side, got down, and low crawled through the shattered window, into a mist of swirling filth, dazzling gold in the Humvee headlights. Wedged beneath the crushed dashboard, I discovered a pair of binoculars, again US military issue. This made me angry, because it meant I couldn't just ignore everything, couldn't pretend that we never stopped, handcuffing me to this wreck, this body. I yanked violently on the binos, trying to free them from the dashboard, when those feet gave a sudden kick. The toe of the gold disco shoe cracked me hard in the temple.

I panicked, reversed out of the truck cab, catching every piece of broken glass and jagged metal on the way out. Bleeding, I scurried backward from the truck like an armadillo hauling ass across a parish highway, finally collapsing onto my back, gulping cold night air.

I lay there, staring at the sober sky, no sound but Lars Ulrich's drum thump on the big desert silence. I wiped my face with my sleeve, force myself to breathe. I finally got my shit together, let loose a stream of contemptuous spit, and went to find Vargas.

Vargas stood over the formerly dead Haji, his hands half-raised, as if he wasn't entirely convinced it was a good idea, his holster empty. Vargas's .45 was in the Haji's shaking hand and aimed somewhere in the vicinity of Vargas's balls, the man cursing wheezily in Arabic. How the Haji got hold of Vargas's .45, we'll never know, because we'll just . . . never know. Shit like that just happened over there. All I know is that Vargas's eyes were fastened to the Haji like a sideshow hypnotist, as if he might will the weapon from his hand. But just in case, Vargas barked over his shoulder:

"Shoot him."

I brought my rifle up, stock planted reassuringly in the valley where shoulder meets chest, as I'd been trained, and sighted down at the Haji.

"Fontenot . . ."

I squeezed the grip and shivered, my thoughts reeling back to late January, when Iraqi armor crossed into Khafji and my rifle was in the same position, combat sling tight on my upper bicep, constricting the flow of blood like a tourniquet, the cold tingling in my arm strangely sooth-ing. Yet I felt like a fraud. Not only was I terrified of being blown up or crushed by those tanks, but I was scared that I'd actually have to use that rifle, to point it at another human being and pull the trigger.

I was getting out of here someday, getting out of the Suck, going home to my ESPN and my Weber gas grill. Not like the poor fuckers we saw on the flatbeds head-ing south, prisoners, completely unguarded, not even re-motely a threat, who sat on the back of the truck, staring out at the desert. They were *fucked*.

One prisoner, who I've always remembered as "the Jazz Singer," stood with his back to the truck cab, wearing a wrinkled blue pinstripe suit and white dress shirt, open at the collar, smoking a cigarette like it was medicine, his vaccine against the shit. The rest of the prisoners, on see-ing us, began cheering and waving, flashing thumbs up. They wanted nothing to do with fighting. But the Jazz

Singer just looked at me as they passed, barely turning his head, eyes full of envy and contempt as he pulled on that cigarette.

"Fucking shoot, Fontenot . . ."

The Haji's arm shook—the pistol waving unsteadily between Vargas and me. I sighted the rifle, center mass, the man dress blazing bright in the light of the Humvee. In my mind I heard the familiar *thwack* of the M16's report, echoing in the empty desert, and saw the man dress blossoming red like wine spilled on a white tablecloth as the round impacted.

"*Do it.*"

I took a deep breath. Relaxed. Aimed. Took up the trigger slack.

But in that moment, as the trigger tightened beneath my finger, it seemed as if everything I'd lived up to that point—the lies, the bad blood after my sister died, who nobody talked about, as if she'd never existed, my father's disappearing act and the divorces, the whole angry raggedy mess—crystallized for me, making a kind of sense, for the first time, as freeing as it was terrifying. I could do whatever I wanted.

I lowered the rifle from my shoulder and stepped in front of Vargas, between him and the barrel of the pistol.

Crouching, I gently touched the Haji's shaking forearm, careful not to betray my own unsteadiness. Almost tenderly, I took the pistol from his hand.

"It's empty."

Vargas snatched the .45 from me, rammed the slide back, staring down the barrel, confirming that it was actually empty. He hit the slide stop and jammed the pistol into his holster, crossed his unforgiving arms, and stared off into the nothingness. I turned to the Haji. We regarded each other wearily, his eyes fighting to stay open, like a small boy struggling to stay awake beyond bedtime, clearly exhausted. From my cargo pocket, I removed a bottle of water I'd gotten at the dump, the only English words being a tagline inviting us to *Taste the Rain*. I unscrewed the cap and tilted the bottle toward the dying man. Water filled his baked mouth. He gagged, spewing mucous and water from his throat and nose.

This startled Vargas out of his mood, handing me the torn utility T-shirt he wore around his neck as field scarf. It was filthy. I wetted the shirt with water and gently wiped the sweat and crud from the Haji's forehead and eyes. He took a deep breath, wincing as his body settled painfully, as if testing the ground he'd soon become one with for suitability. Once more I put the bottle to his lips, and he managed to wet his mouth, his Adam's apple bobbing as he swallowed. His eyes grew heavy, closing to slits, and his breathing slowed, until, finally, he became still, the light from the Humvee headlights in his half-closed eyes.

The music from the boom box ended, and except for the rattling of the Humvee's diesel engine, the desert, and for all I knew the entire planet, plunged into sharp silence. Not knowing what else to do, I folded the damp scarf into a kind of pillow and placed it under the Haji's head. The Humvee was idling rough—time to have Motor T replace the spark plugs, I thought. As I shifted my weight to spare my aching knees, I noticed a familiar red and white pack in the gloom just outside the glare of the headlights, a pack of Marlboro 100s—flip top. One of those mundane witnesses to tragedy, those crumbs from life's big feast. I'm a casual smoker, mostly when I'm drinking, and because of our obsession with being good guests here in the Kingdom of Saudi Arabia, I hadn't had a beer, and therefore a cigarette, in almost a year. But a cigarette, especially a Marlboro 100, seemed like a great idea right then. I opened the pack, it was fresh, the cellophane still on and everything. I removed two, only to discover they were both bent. They all were. I handed one to Vargas. He lit up and handed me his lighter. I placed the twisted cigarette in my mouth, fired up, and tossed the pack back onto the ground and stood, exhausted, my knees burning. I took a deep drag, exhaling into the biting air, looked down at the man, and knew he'd be dead before the sun rose.

But not by me.

A Good Dream

Lance Corporal Gibbs hadn't laid waste to anybody, hadn't liberated anything—with the exception of a tub of rainbow sherbet lifted from the back of the Baskin-Robbins van, devoured with Montague and Lance Corporal Colón in the dank S-4 bunker, like dopey kids at a church social.

While the rest of the Marines "did bad things to bad people"—as battalion commander "Mad Mike" Madigan prophesied with what he hoped sounded like godlike certainty—Gibbs spent the "Mother of All Battles," the so-called showdown between Allied and Iraqi forces during the Persian Gulf War, playing dominoes and eating sherbet.

In theory, Sergeant Travis was Gibbs's boss. Theories are, though, by definition, a kind of wishful thinking, a hope or dream of the way things "should" be, yet at the mercy of human sentiment. "The heart wants what it wants," Montague would sometimes quote Emily Dickinson as they'd try and make sense of their seemingly nonsensical women back home. But he could've been talking about Travis.

Not imposing or handsome enough to be called a "poster Marine," Travis's appearance nonetheless suggested consistency and competence and, for a certain kind of person, attractive in its own right. His hair, mustache, and uniform were strictly "by the book," exceptional for their lack of exception. Yet it was in his eyes, clear and kind and popsicle-y blue, that lay his exceptionalness, that betrayed something deeper, a shyness maybe, as if his eyes were embarrassed by their inability to conceal truth, fueling a ready smile that hid more than it revealed, like a smoke grenade.

Normally watchful and sober—and since his divorce lonely—Travis was given to nights alone, listening to Garth Brooks's first album on cassette, a cigarette burning thoughtfully in his hand.

Gibbs, undeniably, was a blind spot for Travis. Beyond all logic, Travis was somehow disarmed, even charmed, by Gibbs (though he'd never admit it and would never use that word). The objective became subjective. Travis's world was turned upside down by Gibbs.

In contrast to Travis's ascetic, Gibbs was a free spirit, floating through life with all the direction of an airborne seed, seemingly without worry or thought of consequence. Travis worried for the both of them. It was a relationship fit for a *Looney Toons* cartoon, with Travis playing the family bulldog, tasked with safeguarding Gibbs's stray kitten, who purred contentedly as he stepped onto the tightrope, oblivious to the disaster lurking below.

The end of the war hadn't eased Travis's worry any, a tightening noose of anxiety and mishap, as collisions, crashes, and suicides snatched Marines daily. As far as Travis was concerned, there was nothing even remotely heroic about being run over by another Marine in a five-ton truck. Bottom line: Saudi was bad news, even if nobody was shooting at you.

One day, while the desert shape-shifted around them, going from frozen to scorching over the course of an afternoon, Travis and Gibbs stumbled upon two camels fucking in the scrub just off the highway. They pulled their Humvee into the dirt, lit cigarettes, and watched as the male awkwardly mounted his mate. The animals grunted noisily, nipping one another with their huge teeth.

"Ol' girl like it *rough*," Gibbs observed.

Travis dragged on his cigarette, appraising the camels: "They're the only ones gettin' any out here." He smiled his South Carolina Sunday-school smile.

"Shit. Only women I seen here was wearin' *sheets*— hustled into the back of a big-ass Benz. Like she bein' *kidnapped*."

"They got all flavors of WMs down at the port," Travis joked self-consciously, referring to "women Marines."

"I said *women*, dawg!" They broke up laughing.

"Hey, man, get a picture of me." Gibbs handed Travis a disposable camera and walked cautiously toward the straining camels. He struck a pose, standing in profile, unsmiling, his arms crossed over his chest, calling out: "Yo! I look like Chuck D?" Gibbs made a pained face, somewhere between a pout and a grimace.

"You look like a *pendejo*," the term picked up from the Spanish speakers in the battalion. To Travis and his "raised right" sensibilities, *pendejo* was far more palatable than its seemingly cruder English-language cousin.

Travis snapped the picture, motioning for Gibbs to join him.

Gibbs ignored Travis, flicking his cigarette, the camels barking as it showered them in spark and ash. There, scattered on the ground, beneath the hooves of the dancing beasts, lay what looked like sinister billiard balls, uniform, and dark. Travis pulled anxiously on his cigarette as Gibbs moved closer for a better look.

"C'mon, Gibbs. Leave 'em be . . ."

The male warned Gibbs off with a snap of its powerful jaws, as if he *knew*, like some mythic beast of prophecy.

"He munches your junk, I ain't cleanin' it up." Travis smiled, embarrassed by the vague panic prickling his insides. Shielding his eyes, Travis watched as Gibbs walked toward the carpet of green metal balls—the noon sun reflecting dull and grim off their smooth surfaces. *Hand grenades*. Hundreds of them. Travis went cold.

Travis should have said something; the Marine sergeant should have taken charge—but he couldn't help but indulge Gibbs even as a familiar anger flared within him, distilling itself into a kind of self-pity, an overwhelming sense of unfairness rising in his gut. Why him? Couldn't he just enjoy his cigarette? Instead, Travis turned toward the Humvee, grinding his own half-smoked cigarette into the dust. *Gibbs*.

The big diesel engine coughed awake, like a smoker rising in the morning, before settling into a ragged idle.

From the driver's side window, Travis waved impatiently, a fresh cigarette in hand: "C'mon, man! *Vamanos.*"

Gibbs eyed the camels like a runner leading off first. Though they looked ridiculous, stumbling on swollen, arthritic legs, roaring at one another, the male drooling a river of frothy saliva onto his mate's scabby head, those camels would *fuck you up* if you weren't careful.

But "Fortune favors the bold," right? Wasn't that what Mad Mike always preached?

Gibbs was off in a Road Runner dust cloud of arms and legs—*beep! beep!*—snatching two grenades from the dirt, the camels barking angrily as he ran off giggling and breathless. Travis watched as Gibbs stashed the grenades in the cargo pocket of his utility trousers, all half-assed stealth and a rabbity smile, almost daring him to say something. But Travis said nothing.

At Manifa, the division bivouac, a sun-bleached tent city clinging to the sandy crust running along the Persian Gulf, Travis walked in on Gibbs as he stuffed a cigarette carton, loosely wrapped in a poncho liner, under his cot, startling them both.

Travis looked around, as if doing a routine inspection, blandly inquiring, "You good to go, Lance Corporal?"

"Good to go, Sergeant." Gibbs shook his head and smiled absently. "Them camels, man . . . *damn.*"

"I'll not unsee that." He laughed self-consciously. "No sir." Travis caught Gibbs's brown eyes, full of light and warmth, both smiling to cover their embarrassment. "Oooh-rah, Lance Corporal," Travis ended the exchange.

Oooh-rah, that all-purpose Marine phrase, a guttural sound expressing everything from enthusiasm to bitter sarcasm.

The following morning, after the tent had cleared for work details, Travis discovered Gibbs sitting on his cot, admiring the grenades, their heft and undeniable potency. He could almost hear the stories Gibbs spun to himself, of how he came to lay hands on *actual Iraqi grenades*—believing them more each time he told them. *Say something,* he thought to himself. But again, Travis let it pass, the intervening twenty-four hours making it infinitely harder to unfuck the mess he'd created. As he left the tent, a kind of willful ignorance took hold—rooted in a lurking sense of embarrassment over his "un-Marine-like" behavior and the curious power Gibbs had over him. Travis soon forgot about the grenades.

A week later, the battalion headed to Naval Air Station Jubail, a jarring three-hour truck ride to the south. After eleven months, it was finally time to say *"Adios, motherfuckers"* to this wasted sand trap of a country. They were going home.

▲

Gibbs threw up somewhere over the Atlantic. Shannon Airport, in Ireland, had been a party; everyone, Travis included, drank his share of Guinness and Irish whiskey. Never much of a drinker, Gibbs was particularly polluted, unblinking and careful in his movements, a faraway, almost muddy look in his normally bright eyes. Instinctually, Travis kept an eye on him, good "mother hen" that he was. Gibbs rose unsteadily from his seat, death-gripping the headrest. He examined his shirt blouse, wrinkled and wet with secondhand booze and his Cup o' Noodles breakfast. They wore new uniforms, boots and all—issued only hours before they'd boarded the aircraft. Mad Mike demanded his Marines return home looking like *warriors*— and that meant desert camouflage, not the *goddamn tree suits* they'd shown up in. Lieutenant Keane, along with Gibbs and Travis and a bunch of other knuckleheads— bored of waiting in line, burning shitters, and fighting each other—camouflaged their faces and launched a "raid" on a National Guard unit the night before, spitting curses and laughter at the Guardsmen as they drove off, almost a thousand new desert uniforms in back.

Gibbs removed a battered pack of Kools from his breast pocket, shaking loose a cigarette, staring at it guiltily before finally placing it into his mouth.

Did he dare?

Rooting through the overhead bin, Gibbs searched his seabag for his lighter—knees buckling as the big jet hit turbulence. They dipped, the engines making an unsettling sound, pennies being dropped into an air conditioner, the aircraft bowing slightly. Gibbs's hands, slick now with booze sweat, fumbled with the bag's metal clasp. A vein throbbed on Gibbs's forehead; he closed his eyes, tightened his grip on the overhead bin, as if in prayer: *one cigarette, Jesus, one fuckin' cigarette—and I'll be able to make it through this.*

Travis watched Gibbs nervously. From the row behind, he could smell whiskey oozing from Gibbs's pores, the burnt diesel from that morning's bonfire of old uniforms on his skin. Gibbs's face was like high-viscosity motor oil, slow moving and dense, basted with the grease of anxiety, adrift in a reptilian daydream, somewhere between fucked up and hungover.

The plane continued roller-coastering, jolting left and then right. Marines bounced awake, spit cups spilled, gear crashed out of bins. Someone vomited. The aircraft bucked, like a bull trying to throw its rider. Someone whooped a dizzy *Yee-ha!* and laughed. Another Marine let loose. And then another.

The aircraft captain, in the flat twang unique to cowboys and astronauts, made an announcement requesting everyone take their seats. This was punctuated with a bored chuckle, as if the turbulence was good fun. Travis's head pounded, hating the captain. He closed his eyes— hoping all would somehow be better once he opened them again. A nasty bump sent Gibbs crashing to the aisle. The mouth of his seabag hung open in the overhead, as if it, too, threatened to vomit.

Gibbs evil-eyed the seabag. He picked himself up and fell into his seat. Digging into a cargo pocket, Gibbs discovered his lighter—a white disposable, bought from one of the shadowy Pakistanis selling tinny Michael Jackson cassettes and "Time to kick Saddam's butt, man!" bootleg Bart Simpson T-shirts, from the backs of battered pickups at Manifa. On it, a cartoon George Bush, dressed as Rambo, stared back at him. A bandolier of ammo wreathed Bush's bulging neck, an M60 machine gun cradled in his ripped arms. *AmBUSHED!* in big block letters. Gibbs studied the cartoon as if there might be some secret wisdom, some relief from his present misery, hidden there. Hands shaking, Gibbs brought the lighter to his cigarette. The flint sparked—but there was no flame. Gibbs tugged at the wheel, harder now, the flame stubbornly refusing to appear.

Sand had been their one constant the past eleven months. Not the spring-break sand of Fort Lauderdale or Waikiki, but the sand of the Devil himself, razor sharp, closer in texture to dried blood than the stuff pouring like sugar between supermodel toes in *Sports Illustrated*. Sand that got into everything.

AmBUSHED! President Rambo mocked Gibbs, bitterly thinking: *When was the last time ol' Bush dug sand outta his ass?*

The plane bounced across the sky, waking Travis from his fog. From between the seats, he watched as Gibbs banged the lighter against the tray table, the cheap plastic threatening to come apart in his hand. And, as if his prayer for mercy had been answered, the wheel spun easily, Devil sand exorcised, free now to insert itself into an eyeball, a rifle chamber, or even the engine of the aircraft. The cigarette blazed, the dry tobacco crackled. Gibbs inhaled gratefully, lungs filling with sweet Virginia smoke. His shoulders relaxed.

"I know that ain't a cigarette burning on my aircraft." Travis's voice hit Gibbs like the crack of a whip. "The smoking lamp is *out*, Lance Corporal."

Enough was enough.

The aircraft bucked as Travis stood, steadying himself on the headrest, trying to appear unaffected. Whether

draining oceans of soju in a Korean whorehouse, endur-
ing ice storms in the Sierra Nevada, or simmering in the
Saudi desert, Travis never appeared affected. Sober as a
damn judge, always. Gibbs stared blankly at Travis, the
cigarette smoldering in his hand.

"Put the cigarette *out*, Lance Corporal." Travis took
in Gibbs's vomit-soaked blouse, his nose wrinkling in
disgust. He resisted an impulse to clean Gibbs, looking
around guiltily, as if everyone knew what he was thinking.
A flight attendant's worried announcement—*Please take
your seats*—refocused Travis.

"You're a goddamn lance corporal of Marines, Gibbs,"
cursing now to make sure Gibbs understood things were
different. Yet Gibbs continued to stare, his eyes dull
smears. Travis reached for Gibbs's yawning seabag, con-
tents threatening to dump on the deck.

"C'mon, Gibbs," he said, softening despite himself.
"Please."

The aircraft dropped, hurling Travis backward. He
landed heavily, between rows of brand-new boots. Gibbs's
seabag slammed to his chest and burst open, gear bounding down the passageway.

Among the cassette tapes, pilfered desert boots in different sizes, as if to shoe a family, and an unopened tub
of shea butter, a familiar cigarette carton, shades of cool
green, as in a garden, tumbled out, hitting the deck—
hard. A familiar pair of metallic balls broke free from the
carton and pinballed down the aisle.

Travis watched as the little spheres bounced mer-
rily away, as if trained to do so, performing a kind of

choreographed dance, just for him. One in particular demanded his attention, as it ricocheted in the tightly packed aircraft, spinning wildly into the air, like Daffy Duck with a stick of TNT up his ass.

Time slowed, as they always say it does, the confirmation of this fact surprising Travis. He did not think of his ex-wife, his family back in South Carolina, or his many perceived misdeeds. His life did not pass before his eyes. Instead, Travis journeyed deep inside, to his truest self—a place of love.

And from that quiet place, a place of undeniable authenticity, Travis looked up at Gibbs, seeing him as never before, his eyes warm and brown, lit now with an uncommon light, seemingly just for him. In those eyes, Travis saw Gibbs as he surely must have looked as a young boy, not that many years ago. A kind of prince, or god maybe, or God itself. And oddly, the emotion Travis felt wasn't fear—it was *trust*. And from that trust a strangely comforting thought bloomed in Travis's mind, a stillness, an overwhelming peace, as in a good dream:

Gibbs . . .

Surrender

Above the too short couch, the curtainless window exploded in white light, the winter sun flooding the small living room. In the other room, a bedroom with a set of French doors dividing the space, he heard Gordon rooting through his possessions, cursing. Francis buried his face in the cushions.

"Stop making so much goddamn noise."

"I'm looking for my satchel."

"Americans don't carry *satchels*."

Francis burrowed beneath his Marine-issue "all-weather" coat—like the trench coat Bogart famously wore as melancholy cantina owner Rick in *Casablanca*. He'd been using it as a blanket since his discharge the week before. Gordon flung open the French doors and loomed over the couch, a scarf around his neck, like some B-team poet.

Francis removed the coat from his face, took in Gordon and his satchel. "They make those for men too?"

Gordon ignored him. Instead, he said, "Would you mind heading over to Lily's this morning? The guy who runs the halal cart on Eighth and Twenty-Third has been harassing her."

Francis sat up.

"Some Egyptian. Or something. Last week, she's leaving for work, he *follows* her, making this sound with his teeth—a sucking sound." Gordon demonstrated. "Some Egyptian thing. Anyway, the other day? He cornered her in the doorway of her building."

"Call the cops."

"Because he's Arab?"

"Because he's harassing her."

"As if the cops would do anything. Welcome to New York."

"Have a little talk with him then."

Gordon made a sound midway between a laugh and a snort, as if this were the most preposterous suggestion in the world. "I have to be at Pratt by 7:30. I'm teaching. Anyway, I can't just threaten everyone who looks at Lily funny."

"Ah. You want *me* to threaten him."

Gordon sighed with practiced exhaustion. "No. I didn't say that. You were just in the Gulf. I thought you might have some . . . expertise, whatever."

"I have no expertise."

Francis lay back and squinted at the blank sky. A not unpleasant image of Lily in her junior-partner uniform appeared: pinstripes, stockings, heels. Professional. Just this side of brusque. Brains too. The *whole megillah*, as his father would say. Gordon's voice, infused now with a theatrical impatience, interrupted Francis's vision.

"I have to go. I'm late."

Francis stretched as Lily and her junior-partner uniform dissolved into sparks of light.

"He speak English?"

"Don't you speak some Arabic?"

"Yeah. I can say 'Hands up.'" Francis raised his hands in mock surrender. "*Erfah edak.*" The image of Lily crackled stubbornly in Francis's head, a campfire refusing to die.

"Maybe I'll head over there." The bony finger of a tree branch tapped against the window like an accusation.

▲

The wind struck Francis as he stepped onto Eighth Avenue, leaving him momentarily dazed. He looked for the World Trade Center to orient himself, the buildings sparkling and wavy bright through tear-filled eyes.

The halal cart, somehow smaller and more pitiful than he'd imagined, rocked in the gusts, perfumed with bacon grease and river bottom. The sidewalks were choked with New Yorkers, grimly getting where they were going. Francis marched toward the surprisingly delicate cart, wondering how it survived such an environment. Covered in pictographs—chicken and rice, lamb and rice, lentils and rice—like modern hieroglyphics, it glowed fluorescent in the sober gray. He rehearsed possible speeches in his head, stopping abruptly: Why was he doing this? That Gordon had been manipulating him crossed his mind. It wouldn't be the first time. And then he thought of Lily, thrilling at the promise of her gratitude.

Inserting his face into the small window, Francis startled to discover not the leering reptile he'd imagined, but a youngish woman, an expectant look on her face.

"May I help you?" She raised a perfect eyebrow. This woman was *beautiful*. Struck dumb, Francis managed to point at a coffee-and-bagel combination, studying the pictograph as if it held meaning beyond "Enjoy a cup of Good Morning!" She poured his coffee. Handed it to him. No-nonsense. Matter-of-fact.

"Very hot. Be careful." Her English was precise, her warning vaguely maternal, affecting in a way Francis couldn't quite place. He imagined her studying a book of English grammar in between customers. She turned her attention to his bagel.

He held the cup and took a cautious sip. The caffeine hit, giving him the confidence to rest a proprietary elbow on the small counter. He watched her work, her movements graceful in the snug cart, with just enough room to turn slightly left and right. She worked quickly, efficiently, infused with a New York–specific hustle, the ancient enterprise of the immigrant.

Her face was a sovereign bronze, eyes large and impossibly black, of seemingly endless depth, spaced wide, somehow serious and welcoming at the same time, their undeniable intelligence lending a certain nobility to the mundane task of toasting a bagel for a stranger on a cold New York City sidewalk. Aware of his attention, she smiled politely and thrust the bagel at Francis. He flushed and placed his coffee on the counter, as if building a wall to hide behind, and dug his wallet—a collection of credit cards and small pieces of paper, bound by a thick rubber band—from his pocket. He placed the wallet on the ledge, next to the coffee, as he searched for cash.

She watched without expression, the picture of patience. He finally looked up, smiling blankly: "I'm out of cash." Francis searched the cart for something—a sign of some sort, a solution. "Credit card?—got plenty of those." He laughed to signal his unconcern. It would work out— didn't it always? Behind Francis, another customer joined them. *Great*, Francis thought. An *audience*. Wall Street type. Finance douchebag.

But instead of joining Francis's laughter, she merely pointed to a hand-lettered sign: CASH ONLY.

Behind him, Francis heard an exhale of frustration. He turned. The man looked off, annoyed. Francis turned back to the woman. She continued to stare at him, unyielding as brick. Any hint of compassion or empathy or even hope lay stillborn on the sidewalk.

"Well, we've got a problem then."

"Can I just order?"

Francis pivoted to face the man. "Can you just hang on?"

The man stepped back. "Get a job."

"Fuck you," Francis spat and stared at the man, daring him to continue. The man gave a final exhale and huffed off.

Francis felt everything speed up, his brain a car with a bad gas pedal. He took in the cart's name: *King Tut Halal.* Beneath it, a mocking parade of cartoon Egyptians danced stoically. Eyes of Horus watched him, unblinking and judgmental. His thoughts careened to a checkpoint on the Coast Highway. The Saudi guard had smiled at the WM, or "woman Marine," truck driver. Instead of simply waving them through, he made a crude V with his fingers, a "reverse peace sign" as she later described it, simulating sloppy cunnilingus with his swollen tongue— he felt his anger swell.

"Where's the king?"

"Excuse me?"

"The bossman," he said carefully. "King Tut. He around?"

"It is just the name of the cart. King Tut. From Egypt." She cocked her head. "You have no money?"

"No. Did you not understand me? *Bt'ekhkee Englisi?*" *Do you speak English?* He took in her face, her anger giving way to confused hurt. He'd not soon forget that look.

"But where's the guy? Who works here?" Her hand tightened on the bread knife. "You related?"

Her face hardened into an unexpected toughness. In it he saw the past of her Cairo girlhood, her present overflowing Queens apartment, and a future of heartbreak and disappointment that would've snapped Francis in two, like a dead branch.

"My cousin. You have business with him?" She appraised him coldly.

Francis looked away, down Eighth Avenue toward the World Trade Center, unable to withstand her eyes. He briefly thought of apologizing, fleeing to the safety of Gordon's couch. Instead, he plowed forward, like a good Marine.

"My friend's fiancée . . ." Again, a vision of Lily exploded to life. "She lives in that building over there . . ." He nodded toward a colorless Deco building, maybe eight stories, with clean lines, " . . . your cousin, whoever, has a habit of following my friend's fiancée down the street . . ."

She cut him off. "He is in Egypt. The money?"

Francis dismissed her. "You tell him: stay away. Because if I hear otherwise, that he's harassing her? Well, I don't know," he stopped just short of making an actual threat. "That apartment right over there." Francis aimed an accusing finger toward the building. "Understand?" He sipped his coffee. It was cold.

For a long moment there was silence. In the calm, Francis sensed her growing, like a mighty tree, roots taking hold in the cement. And from deep within, something terrible arose, the very fullness of her spirit. Francis retreated into the security of his Marine Corps coat.

"Oh, I understand," she said. "Very well." And smiled.

His cowardice laid bare, he felt dizzy. A kind of drunkenness took hold, almost thrilling in its disregard. Without thought or logic, Francis raised the paper cup in mock salute, pouring his coffee on the sidewalk. He flung the cup with a snap of his wrist. It fled with the wind, down Eighth Avenue. Without any idea of where to go, Francis executed a muddy "right-face," heading in the direction of the coffee cup. He felt her eyes on him, *hating* him.

▲

The following day, as he'd awoken to roaring daylight, the tree branch tapping against the window, the previous morning replayed in his mind. At best, he was an ass. At worst, a bully. Also, his wallet was missing. And it could be only one place.

Francis walked with what he hoped was confidence, down the same loveless sidewalk, past the same trash pirouetting hopelessly, the same impassive buildings, toward the now familiar cart. In his mind, he'd rehearsed apologies, justifications for his behavior, abandoning them as he approached the small window. She looked up from the sink where she washed a cutting board. If she was surprised to see him there, her face didn't show it.

"I was here, yesterday morning," Francis paused, absorbing her stony silence. "I wanted to apologize." He looked at her expectantly. She fixed her head, as if trying to place him.

"I have your money." He held up a five-dollar bill as proof.

She shook her head, wiping her already spotless work area. Then, as if amazed at his still being there, said, "It must be nice. To think so well of yourself. To have everything so easy for you." She indicated her workspace. "Now, please."

Francis shifted, removing a small piece of paper from his coat pocket, carefully pronouncing the Arabic words written in pencil: "*Ana aasef giddan.*" *I'm sorry.*

She looked at him with something resembling pity in her eyes, her laughter filling the small cart. Followed by something in Arabic, something needing no translation. He nodded in agreement, raising his hands in surrender. "*Erfah edak.*"

Francis placed the money on the counter, beneath a napkin dispenser and turned to leave. She watched him go, then leaned out of the cart, waving his rubber-band wallet.

"Excuse me . . ."

Francis stopped and looked up at her. She towered over him, her quiet courage now a kind of beauty in itself. With elbows placed primly on the small ledge, she regarded Francis, shivering before her: "You meant to say: *Ana bastaslim*—'I surrender.'"

Francis's heart beat against his chest. He felt vaguely bound, a rabbit caught in a snare. But Francis was no prisoner, for she had unlocked the cage.

All he had to do was walk out.

Nothing Earth Shattering

She thought about him at the oddest times, the thoughts vaguely embarrassing, as if revealing her to be a fraud—something other than a good wife and mother. She considered herself a practical woman, and by her sober estimation the memories served no purpose. They were, in fact, counterproductive to the already complex task of simply living her life. Yet, as much as she tried, she was powerless to control them. That was the maddening part—their unpredictability. When they were upon her, a kind of *déjà vu* took hold, leaving her unsettled and lost. Like the time two summers ago, on a family trip to Nags Head, when memories of a long-ago beach welled up from the bright sand like a guilty confession, leaving her dizzy and lightheaded in the Carolina sun, as her family chattered about her, oblivious. Or while watching TV, when those Marine Corps ads came on, where the Marine pulls the sword from a stone like a young knight, her memories would crackle to life like the lightning filling the sky in the commercial and she'd bite her lip to keep the tears from revealing her. And last fall, when the Piedmont Gas man lit the pilot light in the floor furnace of their house, the masculine tang of Old Spice and clean sweat lingered long after he'd left, and she sat in the creeping autumn dusk savoring the scent until the smell of burning dust gradually overcame the memory. She hated the power these memories had over her, hated the way they made her feel. But her feelings—if they could be called that— were fleeting, vanishing into nothingness like the pilot light smothered by the October breeze. If she were being honest, she couldn't even remember what he looked like. Sort of pleasant and blond with a nice smile, if she had to guess. She hadn't known him too well. That was a long time ago, she'd tell herself. She was forty-two now. Three kids, almost grown. A decent-enough husband. A nice-enough life.

▲

Lance Corporal Larsen was having the time of his life, living the grand adventure of war. He'd fantasized about his unborn children and the stories he'd tell them. Of how the old man helped take out "the dictator," a family epic for a family that didn't yet exist. There wasn't even a girlfriend, just a girl from back home he'd flown out to Hawaii for the Marine Corps Birthday Ball the November before they deployed to the Gulf.

▲

She'd been out of North Carolina only once, when she was small, to visit cousins in Roanoke, not much of a trip. So Hawaii was a dream come true—the trip of her young life. They'd spent their time doing touristy things: a visit to the *Arizona* Memorial, buying three-for-ten-dollar T-shirts at the Aloha Flea Market, and dozing in the November sun on Waikiki Beach. And that dress-blue uniform, like something from the movies! Erik Larsen was a nice guy for sure. No pressure—not even remotely serious. They'd just kissed.

▲

Larsen, by all accounts, had the world by the ass. Thirty days' paid leave. Full medical and dental. Three squares a day, as his old man always said. And if he ever got time, classes toward his associate's degree at the Camp Hansen branch of Central Texas College in Okinawa. (*Go Eagles!*) He had what any nineteen-year-old, especially a recent graduate of West Pamlico High, would consider a lot of money, direct deposited—minus an allotment for his mom—every two weeks, whether his days were spent pitching quarters and drinking MGD in the barracks or taking on Saddam's Republican Guard. It was all the same to the Marine Corps. Sure beat the shit outta wiping down the soup and potato bar at the Golden Corral.

Before dawn on the day the ground war kicked off, Larsen stepped into the breach, nervous and excited. Though displaying an outward cockiness, Larsen secretly worried about a chemical attack. But Gunner McKee had put on an Oscar-worthy performance the night before, making the men laugh with his dirty jokes, coolly telling them they had nothing to worry about, that they'd be remembered as long as there was a Marine Corps and a United States of America, a speech lifted from the movie *Full Metal Jacket*. *Oooh-rah!* they'd barked at Gunner McKee.

And Gunner McKee hoped he was right.

▲

Larsen was the only casualty that day.

Word spread from Larsen's squad to the platoon, to the company, and then on to battalion. The Marine Corps would send someone to his mom's place outside Raleigh, right? Or was it Rocky Mount? She moved around a lot. His dad? Well, he'd find out somehow. The others, the corporals and the sergeants in the battalion, wondered what the hell Larsen's NCOs were thinking. How'd they let Larsen get away with hanging grenades from his flak jacket by their pins?

"Kids . . . ," they said, though they were only four or five years older.

To Captain Blizzard, Weapons Company CO, it was Darwinism, pure and simple: "Life is tough, tougher if you're stupid." They shot looks over their shoulders and chuckled knowingly, making figure eights in the grit with their boots, launching dip spit onto the littered tarmac of smoldering Kuwait City airport.

But "Mad Mike" Madigan—Larsen's battalion commander—was pissed. Some pansy journalist from *Esquire* had attached himself *like a deer tick on dog balls* to Larsen's platoon when it happened, probably put Larsen on the cover, make him into some big goddamn hero. Cost

Mad Mike his promotion; his regiment too. He'd worked too hard, given up too much, to let it all piss away now.

As he simmered, Mad Mike drained a warm can of Coke, fortified with Wild Turkey, a kindness from the AT&T guys at Manifa, where it was always happy hour. His cheeks, his acne scars, burned, as they did when he drank. Through a blackened hole in the departure-lounge window, Mad Mike watched Marines posing for pictures in front of a wasted jumbo jet, their hands upraised in "devil's horns," saluting the chaos they'd wrought. Silently, he vowed to hang Larsen's platoon commander's balls from the rearview of his pickup for fucking him.

His head throbbed, beyond mere headache. This went deeper. For a brief moment, as the tiny voices chattered, unintelligible, *what were they saying?* Mad Mike felt a familiar panic surge within him. And though he told himself he'd never do it, he understood a .45 round as a solution—a messenger of peace, an exit. And that knowledge, that *intimacy*, terrified him. He felt strangely tired and closed his eyes, leaning his forehead against the cool window. He wanted to shed his uniform, like a snake's skin, and to sleep naked for a very long time. A dim room. Clean sheets. The hum of an air conditioner. The touch of an understanding woman. Not even sexual—a mother maybe. And the realization all of that was so far away. He opened his eyes. It was all still here.

Mad Mike turned up the Ozzy on his Walkman, and tossed the empty can onto the runway below.

"Cocksucker."

▲

Rumor ran wild. A Marine from Larsen's platoon swore it was suicide. *Bullshit.* Why not just stick a barrel in his mouth? Like everyone else, like that brother, that dark green from first battalion?

"That was homicide, dawg . . . ," someone said. Young Marines speculated whether Larsen would get the Purple Heart.

"Shut your sucks," Sergeant Travis snarled. "Guy blows himself up with his own grenade, and you're talkin' Purple Hearts? I fear for the future of our Corps."

Pham, his face stung and red by the shrapnel, said he tripped. The grenade went one way. The spoon another. The pin stayed put. Heard him say *Oh shit.* They hit the deck. That was it.

"Oh shit!" They laughed—not even bothering to look over their shoulders.

Whatever it was, it was exciting. It made the experience real. It was a war, right? Somebody had to die. Iraqis didn't count. It was understood that *they* were going to die—by the carload, by the truckload. Hiding under mattresses in the backs of stolen vans. On foot as they ran: *Let's get the fuck outta here*—all legs and arms and a cloud of dust, like bad guys in a B movie when the posse rides into town.

But Larsen was a *Marine.* He counted.

▲

Lieutenant Keane volunteered to help with the mess that was Larsen, more out of curiosity than anything else.

He'd never seen a dead body before and felt that by a certain point in a man's life, a real man needed to see such things. A bucket-list item, if you will. (Not that Larsen was much of a dead body.)

Keane held the garbage bag for Harris, an unlit king-size hanging from his mouth, seemingly defying gravity. As they looked for dog tags, teeth, bone fragments, whatever—Keane thought of his improbable connection to Harris, his *friendship*, the mystery of it. A white kid from suburban Pittsburgh. A Black kid from rural Alabama. A strange and wonderful bond, despite all. And like a great truth—they'd somehow discovered it.

Afterward, they went through Larsen's personal gear. Found the usual stuff: a well-used Victoria's Secret catalog, a fun-size Butterfinger bar that fell apart as Harris broke it in half, and three blurry snapshots: a dog panting happily in a red-dirt backyard, a pale girl on Waikiki Beach, Diamond Head looming and eternal behind her. The same girl, now wearing what looked like a prom dress, with Larsen at the Birthday Ball. Bootleg cassettes bought from the Mama-san who ran the store outside Gate 1 at Hansen: Guns N' Roses, Metallica, a mixtape labeled *For Jennifer* in ballpoint pen. Nothing earth shattering.

▲

Mad Mike wanted a hero letter. It was the right thing to do—and it would cover his ass. The XO wrote it himself: *The expression of grateful comrades for the loss of an American hero, patrolling behind enemy lines in the defense of fredom*. The letter was well received, though the XO had misspelled "freedom." But that was beside the point.

Thoughts soon drifted to the "Welcome Home Hero" free beer surely in their futures, the grateful handshakes, and the problem of how to send an AK home to Berwyn. They came. They saw. They kicked ass.

The world was theirs.

▲

She'd heard the song in passing—through a car window as she cut across the Hardee's parking lot on her way to work: Tears for Fears' "Everybody Wants to Rule the World." She startled. Stopped in the middle of the lot. Her legs wobbled slightly, like the waves of heat rising from the asphalt, lured by the music to a car Larsen had borrowed for the weekend, the song playing on a small boom box that sat on the frayed backseat because the car's cassette player had been stolen. A gentle silence hung between them, sparkling and soft in the late-afternoon light.

The music faded as the car left the Hardee's lot. She took a deep breath and looked to see if anyone had noticed. There was no one. She got her bearings and headed into the white light of the sun.

After all, she was a practical woman.

Sheepdogs

My father punched out Jay, from "Jay and the Americans"—the moderately successful singing group from the early '60s. This occurred somewhere in New York, possibly at a party in the Village. As the blessed event happened before my birth, the punching out of Jay has always been shrouded in dim mythology, a memory of a memory really. When questioned for specifics, all my father would say is that Jay "fucked up."

Yet the story of Jay's penance took root, becoming part of our family DNA, a genetic trait passed down, not unlike my affinity for long division or love of reading. My father's gone now. Agent Orange—his own penance— took him almost twenty years ago. He exists only in memory and in my sense of righteous indignation. We're all just prisoners of our genetics, really.

This isn't to imply that my father was a violent man or that his emotions were tied to his fists—on the contrary, my father was an often gentle and articulate man; as kids, we held hands well into puberty, and he told my brother and me that he loved us, often and unapologetically. He absolutely worshipped my mother. So when he did "punch

113

out" (his preferred term) somebody, it always seemed justified—even "good." For a man of his generation, born into a world where guys who looked like him ran the show without question, he was fairly evolved. Even by today's unforgiving standards, he possessed an unerring sense of what we'd now call "social justice," though such a term would have seemed pretentious to him. It was a simple matter of "right" and "wrong" to my father, the distinction always clear, something felt rather than thought, a matter of intuition. As he saw it, the world was all sheep and wolves—and my father, a sheepdog.

The winter I was eleven, my father took me fishing in Florida. Three fishless days into our trip, we went to a county fair, on the shores of Lake Okeechobee—the air heavy with diesel, spun sugar, and cigarettes. Men with homemade tattoos, knife-wound smiles, and missing fingers and teeth patrolled the muddy sawgrass. My father's eyes brightened, his body stiffened, and his head tilted, like the cocking of a gun. He watched dutifully as I climbed inside rattling cages with names like "Bullet" and "Kamikaze," and played midway games, even winning a goldfish in a globe of cloudy water. Toward the end of the night, I got suckered into "Drown-a-Clown," a game involving shooting water into a clown's mouth while a balloon inflated atop its head. First balloon to break won a prize: the famous Farrah Fawcett poster— her in the swimsuit, head tossed back, smiling that smile.

"I need players, I need shooters. Who got the killer instinct?" the carny's voice droned into a microphone.

There was just me and two others, a teenage couple, entangled in a hormonal knot. The carny running the game wasn't much older than me—but with an already old face and a barely there mustache—wearing an "old-timey" striped blazer, a size too big, like he'd borrowed it, and a fat "Stars and Stripes" bow tie. A Styrofoam boater floated atop his fuzzy head.

"Shooters, shooters—who gon' bust this ol' clown's mouth? Who got the killer instinct?"

My father stood just outside the tent's swampy glow, disappearing into the dark as much as is possible for a three-hundred-pound man. I positioned myself behind my water pistol, red paint worn silver by thousands of sweaty hands. I had zero doubts about beating the young lovers, more interested in each other's tongues than shooting. As the son of a Marine, I knew marksmanship was in my blood. I took aim, a bell rang. My stream of water was machine-gun fire entering the narrow slit of a Vietcong bunker, my Marines pinned down. The couple giggled, their aim poor—clearly, their Marines were fucked—but I held steady; my balloon grew. The carny paced, whacking the countertop with a bamboo cane. I ignored him, punishing my clown, showing no mercy. The balloon popped—I leaped from my pistol. Seconds later, the couple's balloon burst. The carny stabbed his cane at them.

"We got a winner!"

"But I won. My balloon broke first . . ."

"Take a hike, kid."

"But that's not fair. I *won* . . ."

"Get the fuck out, faggot." He raised his cane as if to swat me.

From the shadows, my father revealed himself, his soft yet still dangerous muscles hidden beneath an Iron City Beer T-shirt and too tight Bermuda shorts. He moved swiftly, even gracefully, going straight for the carny. No talking. No threats. All business. My father grabbed the carny's jacket, lifting him from the ground, his forearms bulging. My father's forearms were his "secret weapon," best used, he instructed, for breaking noses. "Just like hitting them with a baseball bat," he'd say—an idea as terrifying as it was thrilling.

"You want I should pinch your head off?" my father asked, strangely calm, as if relieved that whatever bad was going to happen was finally happening. The odd phrasing of his question made it somehow more threatening, a dangerous vestige of his New York City upbringing, like a knife or pistol strapped to his ankle.

"No, sir, I don't think I do . . . ," the carny rasped, his voice like a struck match. His rational answer to my father's irrational question only added to the impact—as if "pinching his head off" was an actual possibility. Humiliation was indeed a complex art.

With a practiced motion, my father tossed the carny onto the bank of clown heads, his boater floating to the sticky floor with surprising delicacy, like a fall leaf. The carny's face pulsed cardiac red, his mustache twitched with shame, offering me any poster I wanted; hell, I could have the Rolling Stones mirrors, the giant pink poodle dog even. My father ignored him, as if he'd ceased to exist, jerking his head toward the dark where we vanished. I was *pissed*—I really wanted that Farrah Fawcett poster.

▲

The YMCA this past Saturday. The whole family, which is yours truly, my ever-pragmatic wife, my son and his big watchful eyes, who just turned one, and my daughter and her big feelings. She's five. We'd just finished ballet class. My daughter spent most of the class staring at herself in the mirror of the dance studio. That about sums up her interest in ballet. It's a phase all girls go through, I think, like the "princess" phase. But like that billboard says, I'm "taking time to be a dad today," and I'm cool with all of that. I've got no agenda for her other than to be strong, make good choices, and do something in life that makes her happy.

So I straddled the driver's seat, maneuvering my son into his car seat. It's like trying to stuff a raccoon into a sack.

"He's just tired," my wife volunteered, anticipating my anger. *No shit*, I thought, but said nothing, not wanting to prove her right. I wasn't looking for a fight—not that day. Not over this. Simultaneously, I tried to sweet-talk my daughter into her car seat. She's looking at herself and that tutu in the reflection of the car. Suffice to say, I'm frustrated. But that's my normal state, so not a big a deal.

"C'mon, honey. Please get in the car . . ."

Only I discovered that she's now sobbing. We're not talking standard five-year-old girl sobbing, related to, say, the "Tuppence a Bag" scene in *Mary Poppins* or when

Brietta is reunited with her parents in *Barbie: The Magic of Pegasus*. (Our daughter makes us leave the room for those.) This is beyond that, a sadness I'd never encountered with her before. To be honest, it scared me—it hinted at the depth of her sorrow and my corresponding inability to make it "right." A hot shank stabbed my heart.

"She's just tired," my wife explained again.

I ignored her, focusing instead on my daughter, wanting her to share her feelings, but not wanting to scare her off by coming on too strong. She can be tight-lipped, like her mom. I want our relationship to be different.

"What is it, honey? What's making you cry?"

A sob.

"Please talk to me . . . ," I plead, not wanting to seem too desperate.

This is followed by another sob. And when I fear that we're headed down a familiar dead end, she sighed, *"Those boys . . ."*

"Boys?" This is an important detail. A trigger word. I don't like men. They're bad enough alone, but when they're in packs? *Sociopaths.* All of them. Maybe even me. But of course I consider myself the exception—that's for someone else, my wife or my daughter maybe, to decide. In my sudden rush of adrenaline, I managed to subdue my son, momentarily distracted by the sight of his big sister crying.

"Where, honey, where are those boys?"

She didn't even look up. Just fiddled with the hem of her tutu and pointed down Schrader, toward Hollywood Boulevard.

"How many, honey? How many boys?"

"Three . . ." Three? *Cowards.*

And with that I jogged up Schrader, toward Holly-wood, not even noticing how out of shape I've become. It's good stuff, this adrenaline. My wife yelled at me: *"No, Francis."* She's angry. Divorce angry.

Ahead, past the intersection, I saw them. Three boys, late teens or early twenties. I recognized their taxonomy, knew their species. It's them. I had no doubt of that. A car honked as I sprinted through the intersection. Ahead of me the sidewalk is wide open, just me and them. I hoofed it now, passed them, and wheeled around, blocking their way. From their faces, they knew who I was and why I was there.

"Turn around." I pointed in the direction of my daughter. "Now."

They get that I've done this before, that it's in my blood. I herded them back toward the YMCA, back toward my daughter, now just a tiny pink blur on the sidewalk.

The boys started talking, offering up excuses. I said nothing. My heart thumped in my mouth—I couldn't speak if I wanted to.

I presented the boys to my daughter, like a conquista-dor back from the New World, with trophies for the queen. My daughter was oblivious, concentrating on blowing her nose into a napkin my wife held. My son, though, was all eyes, watching through the car door, open to the side-walk. My daughter wiped her nose on the sleeve of her tutu, looked up at me.

"Is this them?"

She nodded gravely.

"Do you want them to apologize to you?" She stared at the ground for a moment, nodded again. I turned to them. They apologized. Something made up. Total bull-shit. I didn't care.

"Are you satisfied?" I asked. My daughter regarded the boys, her thumb thoughtfully in her mouth now, aware of a strange new power. Without taking the thumb from her mouth, she nodded. My wife was furious, I might add. But to her credit, she said nothing. I dismissed the boys with a look. *Get lost.*

Driving home, not without reason, my wife refused to speak. My son and daughter slept in the back. Apparently, they *were* tired. My wife would get over her anger—or not, adding it to her growing list of grievances. Most import-ant, though, it's quiet. Finally, she announced matter-of-factly: "I have book club tonight. I need to stop at Trader Joe's." She's a lawyer, a matter-of-fact person. (I swear "book club" is just an excuse to drink rosé.)

Again, I said nothing. Just nodded.

But for the moment, it was just me and my thoughts. I'm not sure why it was so important to chase those kids down the street. Because that's what they were, kids. Not even worth my time. My father would've done the same thing—at least that's what I told myself. My wife's a smart woman. But there are things she simply does not understand.

I love both my kids, but I love my daughter beyond all reason. It's sad, but my son will have to fend for him-self. His moment will come. I have no fear of that. But my love for my daughter is "beyond." I used to feel the same way about my wife, but that's changed. I want my daughter to know that she's loved. And that the kind of love she deserves is the kind that makes you chase three boys down a Hollywood street. I can only hope she finds a guy who loves her as much as I do. Because when she's seventy-five, I'll be gone. But she'll *know*.

But if I'm being honest, it's not just the love—that's only part of it. The part that doesn't make me sound like one of those sociopaths I mentioned. It was a kind of "showing off," I guess, for my daughter. I want to be worshipped, to be looked upon with awe. I want her to mythologize me as a "righter of wrongs," a protector. A sheepdog—like my father. And it was important not only to humiliate those guys, but to do it in front of her. She had to bear witness, had to be a part of it. That's the important part. It's selfish, really.

But if my father taught me anything, it's that I'm gonna fuck her up somehow, right?

Something Hidden

I'll admit it: I loved the way kids smiled when they saw me in between classes, the boom box on my shoulder, blasting the "Cantina" song from *Star Wars*—Benny Goodman as interpreted by space aliens. It was like the soundtrack to a private movie, where I was the Ferris Bueller character, with my own Sloane Peterson, Ferris's girlfriend, by my side, who wasn't only gorgeous, but cool and smart too, who loved Sousa as much as I did. Our marching band was learning the song for a *Star Wars*–themed half-time show featuring Yours Truly decked out in a Darth Vader helmet and cape. I loved being drum major, not just because I loved music, but because it proved I'd become somebody.

In shop class, where packs of boys mishandled an arsenal of saws, sanders, and routers, Mr. Kunkle indulged me, letting me play my music as loud as I wanted. We were making "cracker boats," as Mr. Kunkle put it, speaking in his soft West Virginia drawl. He often used funny words like "meemaw" when referring to our mothers or "possum box" for the glove compartment of a car. Once, during morning announcements, Mr. Kunkle reported that "wrassling" practice had been canceled due to a snowstorm. That cracked us up.

From his perch atop a carpenter's bench, throned in a kind of rough majesty, Pat McDonough asked Mr. Kunkle what a "cracker boat" was—Mr. Kunkle said it was like a serving tray for snacks, but nicer. Pat nodded thoughtfully, as if learning a great truth, saying he thought cracker boats were ships in the "West Virginia Navy." Smiling his funny smile, Mr. Kunkle cautioned Pat not to get "too big for his britches," which of course only made us laugh harder.

Unlike Mr. Kunkle, bald probably even as a teenager, Pat McDonough had perfect hair, like the feathers of some beautiful bird, iridescent, the color of sunlight through a filched tequila bottle. Pat was forever running his hands through that perfect hair, preening over the pleasure of just being Pat McDonough. You could almost hear him purr. Pat was also a junior, a year above us, and an All-Conference running back, his low-watt smirk quickening pulses of popular girls and middle-aged sportscasters equally. All of it reinforcing an undeniable biologic certainty: that Pat was a man, and we were still hopelessly boys.

While I waited my turn on the belt sander, I cranked the "Cantina" song, doing my drum-major schtick—equal parts drill sergeant and Bugs Bunny—that I did to loosen up our band before football games. The steel-drum solo (my favorite part) came on, giving the music its "otherworldly" quality. I was going nuts, big stupid smile on my face, totally oblivious—showing off. Until

I realized everybody was watching Pat—who had my boom box in his man hands, like it was just another block of wood to be tamed, heading toward the belt sander. Pat placed my boom box on the sander, adjusting it slightly—first this way, then that way—until he was satisfied, the music still playing, the trumpet solo now. Then came the sander's shrieks, like Pat force-feeding a Wookie. After a few moments, he removed my boom box from the sander, matter-of-factly inspecting his work, plucking at plastic splinters with his fingers, and went at it again.

By now, the shop smelled like melting boom box, dizzying and hot—and I just stood there—watching. The other guys sneaked looks, laughing at me, the *doomed*, in their little boy voices. Even Mr. Kunkle, hands on his hips and head cocked in that vaguely prissy way he had, as if deciding whether to be angry or not, finally cracked a smile—a dim spark of cruelty in his eyes, as McDonough ground away.

Finally, Pat shut the sander down, the belt skidding to a stop. The sudden silence made the still-playing music sound tinny and small, like I was a horse's ass for even liking it. Pat removed the boom box from the sander, blew plastic dust dramatically from its surface, in great gusts, like some budding deity, a petty Odin, held it to the light, and squinted for imperfections. At last, he nodded approval and strolled toward me, savoring each step, like it was good to be in his body, to feel what he was feeling, as if he'd done a very good thing.

"Here," he said, simply.

And winked.

▲

I guess I was an "easy-target"—the kid with a dragon on my shirt instead of an alligator. Whose dad, a Marine in Korea, cut my hair himself instead of having it cut it at the mall like everyone else. Whose lunch was packed by that same dad who grew up on Spam sandwiches and sheep parts.

Also, I was the "ethnic kid," because my grandparents came to America from what's now known as Lebanon, opening a tavern on Pittsburgh's South Side catering to Lebanese Christians (we're Maronite Catholics) and steel-workers. I remember my *jidu* proudly announcing that J&L Steel's South Side works outproduced all of Germany during World War II, as if he was responsible, his *kibbeh* and *kafta* meatballs somehow playing a part in Hitler's defeat. Maybe there's some truth there, but I do know my dad won a Silver Star at the Chosin Reservoir and lost the tip of his pinky to shrapnel from a Chinese grenade. Which is to say we're true blue—good Americans.

▲

In bio, we were studying the Western honey bee. Reading from the teacher's manual, Coach Auger informed us that a bee's life is short—a couple of weeks at most in summer. That made me strangely sad. But I'd hoped the honey bee saw life as more beautiful, that those summer weeks were somehow sweeter, knowing he was doomed.

Coach Auger explained that not all bees are created equal. Some are drones. Some are workers. And a select few are queens. In her pink Icelandic fisherman's sweater, nicely tight Jordache jeans, and that sun-kissed skin, even in winter, that set off her perfect teeth perfectly—Liddy Pisarczyk was undoubtedly a queen. That would make Pat, Liddy's lab partner, a drone, I guess, whose primary role was to mate with the unfertilized queen. (My lab partner was a kid everybody called "Fungi," who wore a ski jacket even when it was a hundred degrees.) As part of their mating ritual, Pat and Liddy would often share secrets in class, her mouth to his ear, followed by slow smiles and giggles until Coach Auger would bare his teeth, barking "Get a room! Jeez Louise!" and hitch his pants up by the waist. To me, it wasn't a surprise Pat was failing bio—he wasn't exactly a serious student. And it was almost as if Coach Auger was happy about it.

▲

"Behold, the Band Geek."

I stared at my sandwich. Pat dropped into the seat next to me, sniffing the air like someone in a Carpet Fresh commercial.

"What in the actual fuck is that?" he asked, wrinkling his almost pretty nose.

"My dad packed my lunch," I volunteered, hoisting my spaghetti sandwich for Pat's approval.

"Is it a sandwich? Or is it a pasta dish? It's *both!*" Pat chirped brightly, like a Chef Boyardee pitchman. He rubbed my gut appreciatively. "How many wishes do I get?" I'd always been self-conscious about my weight, but still, I smiled gratefully—dizzy on Pat's attention.

"You're Auger's lab assistant, right? In charge of dead fish and gerbils?"

"A bit more involved than that, but yeah," I answered carefully, stealing a look at Pat. A hungry light, almost like a collapsing star, seemingly surrounded him, pulling me in. But I always saw stuff like that.

"Auger ever let you in the back?" His eyes—*dollar-bill green*—studied me, startling in their intensity. Sweat collected along my Marine Corps haircut. I shifted in my seat, knocking into Jeanie Farber.

"Watch it. Fuckface."

I smiled a nervous apology, turning back to Mc-Donough, my face hot. He hadn't taken his eyes—*flecks of gold*—from me. I took a deep breath, conscious of the steady pressure of his hand on my shoulder, as if he was guiding me, leading me to some prearranged destination. It was hard to think.

"I mean, uh . . . I'm his assistant."

"You ever go through his desk?" At first, I thought Pat was accusing me.

"*Never.* Coach Auger trusts me."

"Not even for shits and giggles?" McDonough zeroed in, gifting me a sly smile. We were buddies. Coconspirators. "I bet he's got all kinds of shit in there. And not just confiscated hacky sacks. Know what I mean?" I didn't know what he meant—but found myself laughing anyway.

"Yeah," I nodded knowingly.

"But you could, if you wanted to . . . right?"

"Like I said, he trusts me."

"Rad. You think you could troll the midterm? The master test or whatever they call it? The thing with the answers?" Pat squeezed my shoulder.

▲

It was easy.

After not that much soul-searching, I did indeed get McDonough "the thing with the answers." I *wanted* to help Pat. That "hungry light"—how could I not? Pat not only passed the midterm, but scored a 93—which seemed only to further annoy Coach Auger—raising his grade to an unimpeachable C. That Friday, as if still under the spell of that magical 93, McDonough set a conference record, rushing for almost two hundred yards as Deerfield bulldozed Mingo Creek before a crowd of almost ten thousand. Pat scored two touchdowns, doing his Angus Young AC/DC "duckwalk" across the end zone, like he always did to celebrate. But even within all that madness, Pat took the time to find me in the band, pointing to me from the end zone—*Behold, the Band Geek*—as we started up "Go Bananas," our after-touchdown song. The second time he scored, Pat threw me the football. And though I wasn't expecting it, I caught it. And then they were cheering *me*. As if I'd scored the touchdown. I felt like I'd been knighted.

▲

The following week, it was back to the life cycle of the Western honey bee and feeding the fish and gerbils, as Pat had predicted. Even band felt predictable. But as I stood alone in "the tower," as we called it, yelling about posture and alignment, I had the sudden realization that I'd stolen a test and threw up. Mr. Willard, our band director, made me go home because he thought I was sick.

The next day, fixating on the empty seat next to Pat, where Liddy normally sat, I fantasized about her sharing a secret with me, the recognition in her eyes, drawing me close as she stood on tiptoes to whisper into my ear, her voice hot and husky and sweet, like good whiskey, filling me with her soft urgency. I sat for a moment, knowing the feeling would soon be gone, letting it work through me. And in that moment, feathering his hair with his hands, Pat looked at me—as if he knew what I was thinking—and winked.

▲

That wink stuck with me. Thirty-five years. Lots of life—both good and bad—lived. After years spent with various orchestras around the globe—Bologna, Hamburg, Auckland—I'd just been named guest conductor for the Pittsburgh Symphony Orchestra, a homecoming of sorts and a midcareer "attaboy," as my father would say. Not that I saw myself as a big deal or anything—far from it. Still, it was enough to be inducted into the Deerfield "Hall of Fame" at a semiformal dinner held in the Nutrition Center, followed by a "Parade of Honor" to White Tail Stadium where we were introduced before a football game. As polite applause rippled, our heads bowed with ingrained restraint, a familiar face appeared at the far end of our procession—the "dollar-bill green" eyes, still alive with irreverence and conspiracy, and that Friday-night smirk. Pat put his arm around my shoulders like an old comrade.

Pat had played football at a small state school, but a series of nasty concussions cut his career short. He lost his scholarship. Dropped out. Following guys like my father, Pat joined the Marines. He went to the Gulf. Saw just enough to not want to see it again. Had something they thought might be MS, possibly from the vaccines they'd given him. On bad days he used a cane. But the experience had changed him. He'd been raising "heritage turkeys," of all things, Narragansetts and Bourbon Reds specifically, for the past twenty-five years. "Great personalities," Pat said of the birds, that followed him around "like faithful hounds." I asked about Liddy; Pat said he was in touch for a while, but had lost contact. She'd been a popular TV meteorologist in Dallas–Fort Worth, until her arrest for shoplifting $850 worth of men's wallets from the Neiman Marcus Clearance Center. Her mug shot, he said, was all over the Internet—like one of her breathy secrets gleefully exposed.

Late that night, looking at Liddy's mug shot, I was struck by how time transforms, sparks a slow-burning fuse leading to an almost imperceptible detonation, making the impossible possible. I don't know if I expected an apology or simply an "acknowledgment" of our past from Pat, but it didn't happen. Maybe it didn't matter. Because as Pat and I stood together, against the cold October rail, separating the stands from the field, from who we were to who we are now, our shared history bound us like refugees washed ashore in a foreign land. And though it was unspoken, we were grateful to be there—together.

As I helped him up the bleachers, through an autumnal mist of cigarette smoke, stadium lights, and the blue-sky possibility of youth—that uncomplicated and uniquely American quality—Deerfield scored. The band played "Go Bananas," and the night opened before us, as if revealing something hidden, like the life cycle of the Western honey bee, all the more miraculous for its brevity, like a wink.

In Dreams

Famously, I could fall asleep anywhere, sleep through anything. To the annoyance of my ex-wife, I slept through the '94 Northridge earthquake in LA. Magnitude 6.7—which lasted twenty seconds. She said it sounded like a freight train going through our house. Never woke up. In ninth grade I slept for a *week*; refused to wake. It was either that or—I don't know. The "why" isn't important. Some guys, bullies basically, who I thought were friends, weren't. The usual. But it shook me. I slept my way through it. At the end of the week, my eyes opened, like a spell being broken and I went back to school where, by then, my tormentors had moved on. Nobody said a word. But that feeling, shame, or betrayal, or whatever you want to call it, had become a part of me.

So sleep is some powerful stuff. It's always been a "way out"—a short cut through the woods, because, as Little Red Riding Hood discovered, the woods are a dangerous place.

But I'm still here. And so is Francis.

▲

As kids, Francis and I were bound by an almost feral devotion—brothers, my own kids would say, from another

mother. After we quit football, we'd spend newly free af-
ternoons locked in my attic bedroom, our fortress against
the world, suffocating in summer and freezing in winter.
But weather was *boring*, for squares who watched the 6:00
o'clock news worrying whether to bring an umbrella to
work. We wore shorts, and Vans, with no socks, even in
February, with snow drifts three feet deep, our legs pale
and drained like supermarket chickens. We didn't care.
We'd sneak pot in the attic, listen to punk rock, stage-
dive off my bed with the Road Runner sheets. We'd start
a band, even had a name—"Gay John Wayne"—but not
much else. We'd hitchhike to California. Become Buddhists. Back then, it didn't matter. We knew we were destined for greater things. For the first time in my short life,
I'd found someone who *got* me. And I got Francis. I really
believed that.

Our friendship was born out of an accident, one
of those seemingly insignificant moments that forever
change your life. Coach Auger—with his baby-doll arms
and legs, attached, like mismatched game pieces, onto a
pony-keg body—called me "faggoty Jesus" at football one
day. With my beard and mullet and sometime eyeliner,
I'll admit, I did look "Jesus-like"—"goth Jesus" or "pirate
Jesus" *maybe*—but in any case, Coach Auger hated me.
He loved Francis, though. Everyone did. Which made it
more confusing when Francis—team captain and an All-
WPIAL wide receiver, which in Western Pennsylvania
meant you were a kind of deity, though short-lived, like
a Fourth of July sparkler—basically called *bullshit*. Not
just on Auger and his lazy bullying, but on everything

Deerfield, our *Forbes* magazine "Top Tier Township," offered as proof that we were somehow different, our *exceptionalism*, I guess you'd call it, entitling us to whatever we could get our hands on. It was like Francis had committed treason.

Auger stood over where he'd dropped me with a sucker punch, calling me *faggoty Jesus* and yelling about how he'd "crucify" me, when Francis appeared, his shadow long in the September sun, like the Man with No Name strolling into a spaghetti-western saloon, hissing *Let's go*— as if we were the only two people on that field. I grabbed hold of his hand, which was cool and untroubled, the tips of his fingers transferring something to me, a kind of resurrection maybe, as he lifted me from the turf.

I felt it immediately.

And as if we *were* the only two people on that field, our teammates, coaches, and the chain-smoking dads who'd watch practice every day from the bleachers—simply ceased to exist. We left the field, and as we headed to the locker room Francis grabbed my hand and held it above our heads, as if declaring us winners, of what—who knows? Life maybe. At least, that's how I felt. It was like being anointed. A sign that I'd been chosen.

Francis didn't care what anyone thought, about holding my hand, about anything—he was fearless. And that was contagious. Francis made me feel potent, how I imagined Adam Ant, the English new-wave singer, might feel, whose *Kings of the Wild Frontier* poster watched over my bed, flintlock pistols cocked, like some rogue guardian angel, reeking of sex and gunpowder. And that there was a place for me, beyond football, beyond Deerfield, where I didn't have to pretend. On a family trip to London over spring break, Francis got me a gold skull-and-crossbones earring. It matched his own, a small *vendetta* knife. Our earrings were a statement to the world; *this* was different. *We* were different. I slept in that earring, wore it in the shower even, and my earlobe turned green from the metal.

An earring was serious back in the '80s. A declaration. Francis's dad, a Marine pilot in Vietnam, whom we called "Lord Humongous" after the villain in *Mad Max 2*, would shout *Ahoy!* whenever he saw me, rattling the ice cubes in his cocktail glass, as if laying the country-club equivalent of a voodoo curse on me—before disappearing into the basement game room with its wet bar and freezer full of Stoli.

But if I'd looked closer, Lord Humongous was merely acknowledging another truth, beyond mere confusion, as to why Francis, a straight, overachiever, future valedictorian, and, according to Lord Humongous, headed to the US Naval Academy, had bought me—a (presumably) straight, underachiever—an earring for a gift. That Francis and I were an odd pair, an Orpheus and Eurydice, Leopold and Loeb or a Sid and Nancy—and destined for tears.

▲

Francis came from the Pheasant Run development, with its corporate lawyers, local news anchors and Pittsburgh Steelers, and million-dollar country-club views, whose garage, with its Ski Doos, Sea Doos, and hot tub with drink holders, not to mention the alpine-white Porsche 944 parked there, was bigger than my whole house; nicer too. Then, midway through senior year, Lord Humongous got caught up in an FBI sting, involving bribing state officials to repave the Pennsylvania Turnpike. He plea-bargained, doing two months at Loretto, a federal minimum-security prison east of Pittsburgh. Without ever discussing it, Francis began staying at our house, until finally he was living with us.

At our house, "Anything goes" could've been our motto, like on those wooden plaques at the county fair proclaiming "Free Beer Tomorrow" or "Kiss the Cook." Heading up our home was my mom, whom we called by her first name, Lydia, like bratty kids on some sitcom. To say my mom was one of a kind doesn't begin to do her justice. I *adored* Lydia.

Nor was I alone—far from it. Men had always claimed Lydia, from Mr. Rooney, my Pony baseball coach, who asked her to marry him at every one of our games, to Mr. Scalia, produce-department manager at Giant Eagle, the local supermarket where Lydia was something of a celebrity. Mr. Scalia, a '60s teen idol—like Frankie Avalon gone to leather, or an Egyptian mummy in tinted glasses—courted Lydia with big talk about his fig tree, as if its potency matched his own. Meanwhile, Lydia's new wave red hair (Rit scarlet dye mixed with Sharkleberry Fin Kool-Aid) and vaguely untamable air, like the horses running free on a Bob Seger album cover, meant men couldn't help but fall for her.

But it went beyond mere beauty. Lydia was a celestial phenomenon—a solar flare or a blood moon—yet with an essence very much of the earth and, being one of six kids who grew up in an abandoned railroad shed, also of hunger and want, hidden in the fugitive light of her eyes, in a smile that meant almost anything but pleasure. So at the end of the day, we were all just her willing captives.

Things might've been different if my father was still around, but he died when I was two. Something to do with the railroad. An accident. Cancer, maybe. Lydia didn't talk about it, and that we were ever three—a family—is hard to imagine. It had always been just me and her, and that was enough. I never thought to ask if she was lonely—if it was enough for her.

As if following a story arc carefully mapped out in some LA writers' room, it wasn't long before Francis and I stopped hiding our beer and weed and started sharing it with Lydia—*cue laugh track*! Most days, after school, we'd sit in the TV room huddled beneath the afghan Lydia crocheted in black and gold, Steelers colors, passing my one-hitter between us, watching reruns of *The Addams Family* and *The Munsters*.

As the weed worked its magic, I'd sometimes look at Francis, in a kind of wonder. He'd catch me, and I'd start laughing, like I was just really stoned, but there was obviously more to it. That he chose to stay at our house, with the squirrels in our walls, the back porch falling into the creek, and the Buick Century rusting in the gravel driveway, said much about Francis's family and home life. We were Whiskey Rebellion descendants, semirural people who looked on as the Appalachian foothills we called home slowly gave way to tasteful five-bedroom homes and golf courses. We were rednecks, really—or worse. Depended on who you asked. So Francis's presence validated us somehow, as if a mad prince had abdicated his throne, choosing instead to live with the commonest of commoners.

That spring, our senior year, Francis turned down an appointment to the Naval Academy and Lord Humongous stopped speaking to him, as abruptly and cleanly as if excommunicated. The Gospel of Wealth brooked no heresy. We graduated in June. A day later we headed for Los Angeles in the Buick Century.

It could have been the bright summer morning, heavy with the scent of a something flowering along the sulfury creek behind our house, or her desire to be through with yet another good-bye, but as Lydia saw us off, she had a look in her eyes I hadn't noticed before—a look of shock, or mourning even, the light dimmed, as if ambushed by the actuality of our leaving.

Lydia hugged me tight, then pulled me tighter, placing her head on my chest, her hair smelling sweetly of breakfast—kielbasa and eggs and coffee—an essence I've long associated with love, and said: "Don't become one of those Hollywood assholes."

But when she hugged Francis, she looked into his face, as if seeing something, beyond blessed genetics, pulled him close, kissed him full on the lips, then walked into the house.

▲

Los Angeles was a city of snares, capturing us, as millions before us, in its nets, like songbirds destined for cages. We auditioned—Doritos, AT&T, Kraft singles—you name it. We got jobs here and there, extras in music videos, some student films, once as stars demonstrating proper hand-washing technique in an industrial film for the navy. *Citizen Kane* our films were not. Then, when I began bringing my infant daughter on these auditions, I knew that was it—I'd hit bottom. I quit, cold turkey, like a smoker after a cancer scare.

Wanting to keep our hand in the biz, we began "street casting." Chinese supermarkets, poker casinos, and dog parks became our kingdom. Specific people with specific body types for prescription-drug ads: Korean men between forty-five and fifty with 30 to 35 percent body fat. Same-sex couples with shingles. Albino fraternal twins. An "only in LA" job—which, of course, is a euphemism for "weird." As a friend once said: *You get the LA you deserve.*

Almost twenty years later, I'm still on the streets, casting. Francis sells real estate.

This past weekend, Francis and I flew back to Pittsburgh for Lord Humongous's memorial service. (A golf-cart rollover; the Lord's ashes sleep forevermore with the fishes in the pond off the sixteenth green at Deerfield Country Club.) Afterward, we got high on the couch in the TV room with Lydia, who simultaneously acted as if we'd never left and treated us like returning heroes. Jet-lagged and hungover, I passed out on top of my old bed, Road Runner sheets faded and thin now, in the attic. As I drifted off, straddling the conscious and unconscious, I heard *The Addams Family* theme—*Strange!*

Deranged!—floating up from the TV room like a lone-some spirit, welcoming me home.

I dreamed I lay on a trampoline.

The suburban summer night purred with familiar sounds—a sprinkler, backyard laughter, an ice-cream truck lullaby—cocooning us in sweet warmth, like vodka lifted from Lord Humongous's game-room freezer. Heather, the girlfriend of a friend who'd just moved to New Jersey, lay next to me. She was fourteen. I was thirteen and deliriously—insensibly—in love, high on the peculiar magic of night, making possible what's impossible by day. We faced each other, our mouths close, whispering. Heather's voice was husky, a feline growl that made everything sound vaguely like a challenge. Her hot breath kissed my face, peppery and sweet, like the cinnamon toothpicks we'd dared each other with in school. I inched closer. Our lips touched. Almost.

"You gonna kiss me?" She made it sound like a dare. I desperately wanted to kiss her, but in my dream, I held back, for reasons I didn't fully understand, beyond mere guilt. I knew a kiss was a dangerous thing, a deed that couldn't be undone.

As if sensing this, Heather made a sound, felt more than heard. Her lips, charged and hot and elemental, water boiling on a kitchen stove, burned against mine, kissing me without kissing me. I felt her in my fingers. My toes. My hair. A delicious pressure. To Heather, there was nothing existential about kissing.

"You gonna do it?" she teased.

"Yeah." The word caught in my throat.

I felt her lips curl into a tight smile, pleased by her victory. She tightened against me, as if claiming her prize. A thousand thoughts—that we'd marry, have kids, a family—each as plausible and real as the next, exploded in my head, like dreams within dreams. My heart swelled with foolish joy.

And then Heather was gone. Everything I'd felt was magnified a hundred times by her sudden absence. I knew I'd never see her again.

"Let's go," I heard Francis command from somewhere far away.

I startled awake.

The house was silent. Dirty sunlight cut across the wall. The tree outside my window cast shadows on the wood paneling, the leaves active and alive, almost watchful, a creature breathing as it lay in wait. I panicked, not recognizing my surroundings, as if I'd awoken in a tomb instead of my old bedroom. I was alone, seized by fear. I felt my way downstairs, through ancient shadows, hand trailing dark walls, already hot from the new day. My dream remained stubbornly alive, a dull fog refusing to burn off. Just outside the TV room, I stopped, blinded by sudden furious sunlight from a window. As my eyes adjusted, the house gradually came into focus again, yet somehow different now, as if a hood or veil had been removed. On the couch, Lydia slept with Francis, Steelers afghan binding them, their bodies tangled in the clear summer light, revealing them, like mythological lovers in a Renaissance painting, collapsed onto one another, the way children sleep. I watched for what seemed like a long time, debating whether to wake them. To say something.

▲

I felt nothing. Not anger. Not hate. Not even disgust, which is how you're "supposed" to feel when you discover that your best friend, your brother—how I'd come to describe Francis—is with your mom. Only a mean emptiness, worse than small talk with the camera operator at yet another Taco Bell audition, hoping that it will make a difference, any difference, and knowing it won't.

Back in bed, the sheets rough against my skin, my thoughts drifted to when I'd separated from my wife sometime after that earthquake I'd slept through. I sat in my car, on an unlit LA street, unable to think, my heart full of poison, until, after hours of this, I headed for Francis. Where else would I have gone? Francis took me in, poured me a shot of whiskey—"the good stuff," as he called it, reserved for life's big milestones, the births, marriages, deaths, and now separations that gave meaning to our lives. He made me drink. Made me laugh. Why? Because I knew Francis loved me better than anyone. And I loved him—though I never had the courage to say those exact words, I know he knows it. I believe that.

I turned to the wall, pulling the pillow over my head to block the afternoon light. I felt hidden, safe even, as if I'd discovered a hole, an entrance to something. I could hear my heart beating. Then my thoughts faded until it was again silent, and I drifted into darkness, into dreams, deeper, and then disappeared completely.

The Man behind the Curtain

The first time I saw my father cry, I actually laughed—not that it was funny, but that it was unexpected, as if I'd discovered that Mister Rogers hated kids or that my brother and I had been found in a basket, floating down the Nile, like Moses and, I guess, Aaron—and I wasn't sure how to wrap my head around such a revelation. My father was a giant, not just physically (though he was big) but psychically too. *King Shit, and everyone knows it*—as my cousins would say, as if describing a combination of Babe Ruth, Clint Eastwood, and a ninth-century Irish chieftain—the unshakable center of my (admittedly small) world.

We'd been playing "war" with the McNulty brothers, our next-door neighbors. Old Man McNulty had been a bombardier on a B-17 during World War II. He'd been shot down and taken prisoner during the murderous Schweinfurt raid. That made the McNultys the US Eighth Air Force, as Kevin, the oldest, insisted—the "good guys." My brother Dominic, and I—we were the Nazis. We'd protested that our dad had been a pilot too, in Vietnam, and a Marine. Vietnam "didn't count," according to Kevin, citing some vague hierarchy known only to him.

"Be gone or be dead, you Kraut fucks," Kevin dismissed us with a moist hand, as if waving away a bad smell.

Dominic and I huddled behind the bumper of our station wagon, parked beneath the porch where our dad stored seasonal stuff—storm doors, screens, and Christmas decorations. As Dominic, still a scared kid of five, held to me, we heard a shrill *Bombs away!* as beer bottles, the miniature Miller Hi-Life "ponies" that Old Man McNulty drank by the bushel, shattered on the driveway around us, splattering us in stale beer, like holy water from some profane Irish American blessing. Dominic shrieked, hands clutching his face.

"Run, crybaby Nazi bastards!" the McNultys howled as we sprinted for the safety of our house.

In the kitchen, I watched my mother coolly take charge, flushing glass from Dominic's eye beneath the faucet. My father, an All-American catcher at Fordham and hero Marine pilot, all six-foot-three and 225 capable pounds, stood helpless, pressed flat against the refrigerator, body trembling with sobs, his normally sure hands holding on as if to keep from melting away, like a popsicle dropped on the kitchen floor.

Useless. Borrowing one of his favorite adjectives.

My laughter sprung from the sheer unreality; the dangerous heresy his tears hinted at—that despite his inescapable gravity, my father was not who he'd purported to be—more "Man behind the Curtain" in *The Wizard of Oz*, than "Man with No Name" in *The Good, the Bad and the Ugly*—and terrified of discovery. Still, buried within my laughter, equally unreal and unexpected, like the Virgin Mary appearing to lowly Juan Diego on a barren Mexico City hillside, was the connection his tears implied: undeniable proof that I was my father's son—and not the imposter I feared I was.

My father knew what the world did to boys who cry.

▲

Not long after Dominic's emergency, my father and I sat in the kitchen, our silence sweetened by the scent of eggs and toast and burned coffee, the Saturday-morning smells that forever summon our time together, like incense summoning God during Mass. A model of the *Enola Gay*, the famous Hiroshima bomber, lay in pieces on the table in front of us, exposed like small clues to a much bigger secret. I studied the painting on the model's box. Amid the wreckage of the burning city, a lone *torii* gate, symbolizing the transition from the mundane to the sacred, stood red and defiant in the smoke.

"Are the Japanese Catholic?" I asked. My father, having been to Iwakuni with the Marines, I supposed was an expert on all things Japanese.

"They're mostly Buddhist. And Shinto, I think." I'd heard of Buddhists—my cousin in Queens, who'd shaved her head, and at Thanksgiving one year suggested that maybe grapes had feelings—but I'd never heard of "Shinto." My father explained that Shinto was a kind of "tree and ancestor worship," and that the kamikaze, the World War II Japanese pilots who'd dive their planes in suicide attacks on American ships, were Shinto. He related this with a kind of awe, taking long, thoughtful drags on his cigarette, a sentiment that bled necessarily into the well-known story of my uncle Eddie, a "tin-can sailor" onboard a US Navy destroyer in the Pacific. Eddie had stood mesmerized, as if witnessing some terrible miracle of unknown origin, heaven or hell or both, his Old Gold ablaze, as a kamikaze plunged into the deck of his ship, killing the men on either side of him, while leaving Eddie untouched.

But Eddie, who'd disappear for months at a time, was a "loose grenade" to my father, an embarrassment who couldn't handle his liquor or his emotions. Often, my father would get phone calls from weary Bronx bartenders, tired of Eddie mooching drinks and smokes. He'd then dutifully head, five hours from our home in Pittsburgh, to some forgotten corner of the borough in our station wagon, to collect an always surprised Eddie. Then, after a sloppy reconciliation and settling of tabs, my father would deposit Eddie once again in his Yonkers basement bedroom, where he'd sob himself to oblivion. And rather than seeing just another ruined drunk, whose life had peaked at nineteen at the Battle of Leyte Gulf, there was something about Eddie that was pure, almost majestic, in his inability to be anyone other than himself. I always felt connected to Eddie, with his startled look, like he'd just woken up, and sad, almost apologetic smiles, and the Kennedy fifty-cent pieces he always had for my brother and me. The appeal of Eddie's story was also rooted in the kamikaze, who, as my father explained, lived the Shinto belief that it was the highest honor to die for something or someone you loved, to sacrifice yourself. And Eddie, though he just stood and watched like a rubbernecker at a bad accident, was forever elevated by that sacrifice, like a family saint.

After he stopped speaking, my father watched his cigarette's smoke spiral upward, slowly dissolving, like a stubborn memory, into the kitchen ceiling.

"Do kamikaze go to heaven? If they're not Catholic?" I asked carefully. My father gave warning signs, a certain head twitch, one of seemingly thousands of tics that let me know he was tiring of me and my questions—yet he continued dragging on his cigarette, as if he hadn't heard me. Watching him, I added cautiously, "Mrs. Maitland says the Catholic Church alone possesses the full means of salvation."

"Who?" he said as if I'd interrupted something.

"My 'Ten Commandments and Beatitudes' teacher."

"Oh," my father said, and stubbed out his cigarette. "I guess not then."

"Did you know that it killed two hundred thousand people?" I volunteered.

"What did?" His voice took on a sudden edge. I showed him the *Enola Gay* painted on the model box. Sunlight haloed the bomber's silver skin as it banked, cool and aloof, through the clouds, a towering god fleeing the stench of human suffering wrought below.

"This is the plane that dropped the atomic bomb, right?"

His head twitched.

As if catching himself, he smiled, not really a smile at all, and nodded. "The bomb. It killed two hundred thousand people. Children too," I said, pausing to look at him. "Will all those people, those children, go to heaven? Even though they're not Catholic?" My father pulled his chair closer to the table, making a loud noise as it scraped across the linoleum.

"I don't know, Francis," he said finally and sighed. He looked as if he wanted to say more, but couldn't, for reasons unknown even to him.

"Colonel Tibbets?" I asked.

"Tibbets?"

"The pilot who dropped the bomb." I pointed to the small dab of paint that was the pilot. "Him. Will he go to heaven?" My father nodded again, as if considering this.

"Did you ask Mrs. Maitland?

"Yes."

"And?"

"She said he's going to heaven."

He cleared his throat and said, "So. There you have it."

I watched as he ground the cigarette into the ashtray made from the base of a mortar shell. Brass. Something he'd brought back from Vietnam.

"You dropped bombs on people, right?" I asked. My father closed his eyes for what seemed like a long time. Long enough to discover that his eyelids were freckled.

He answered slowly, measuring his words, as if each was potentially dangerous: "That's what pilots do in war, Francis." His voice sounded thin, a rubber band pulled tight, before it snaps. "They drop bombs on people. Bad people."

I tried to imagine what that would be like. To be on the ground when my father came overhead with a load of bombs—one of the bad people. His chair scraped across the floor again. He went to the refrigerator, nosily rearranging jars and Tupperware. "Three goddamn mustards and no beer," he accused a squat yellow jar. "Who eats all this?"

I knew enough not to answer. After a long moment, he grimaced, as if trying to recapture his almost smile. Instead, the skin of his face stretched pale, almost see-through, exposing teeth, like a snarling dog's. I imagined I could see his bones. The jar fell from his hand, shattering on the kitchen floor.

"Did something break?" my mother yelled from upstairs. My father stood, his shoes and pant legs splattered with mustard.

"Goddamnit." He slammed the refrigerator shut. Jars rattled in alarm. "Three goddamn mustards," he growled. I leaped from the table, a small animal startled from hiding, picked glass from the puddle, and apologized. "Don't apologize," he said and walked off, glass crunching beneath his feet, yellow footprints following him out of the kitchen.

I didn't see him for the rest of the day.

▲

The summer my father coached my Pony baseball team, I discovered I couldn't hit a curveball. No matter how hard I tried, that ball would start curving and I'd panic, hitting the dirt as the umpire called *Strike!* I'd look up at my father, standing on the dugout steps, his embarrassment made infinitely worse through the perversion of my tears. To him—a catcher one summer with Pawtucket, the Red Sox minor-league team—my inability to hit a curveball wasn't just another childhood mishap to be learned from and gotten through; it was a referendum, something any American male ought to be able to do, like changing a tire or undoing a bra. *It's just a game,* the other dads would say, their eyes on my father. *It doesn't mean anything.* But it did. It meant everything.

Yet there were always clues, hints of something else at work, undeniable, just beyond perception. Something like the "mystery of faith," as Mrs. Maitland might explain it.

As Dominic began preschool, painful sores appeared on his face and body, reminding me of a movie we'd watched about Father Damien of Molokai ministering to the lepers. I was terrified of Dominic's extremities falling off. *Psychosomatic,* I remember my mother saying, trying to reassure me. She'd wait until Dominic was asleep to apply the special ointment the doctor gave us. And every night, as she'd dab his face in the dark, he'd wake screaming. My father, finding himself trapped, would escape to the garage, blasting a baseball game or staticky music on the car radio. The next day, rather than getting angry or threatening my brother, my father went to school with Dominic. Eventually, he even took vacation days, eating with Dominic, playing with him, easing him into school, until he was comfortable being on his own. Or, when I was in sixth grade, and Mr. Softley, my homeroom teacher, twisted my arm behind my back, because I'd been "disrespectful" during the Pledge of Allegiance. My father marched into homeroom the next day, pulled Mr. Softley from the model trains he'd paint before the bell, and disappeared with him outside. A few minutes later, Mr. Softley came back alone, with a look like he'd just walked away from a bad car accident unhurt, and apologized to me in front of the class. Or, years later, when I was a Marine myself—not a very good one—and my father called me long distance in Okinawa to tell me that Dominic was HIV positive and sick—more sores—as if confirming my leprosy fears. But what I remember most is my father's voice, lost and small over the miles, filled with such sadness, as if he'd realized all the world was capable of. And though he never said the words, I knew my father loved us. But always on his terms.

▲

Years later, during a maddening run-in with insomnia, I'd often sit in my son's room, watching him sleep, like an alcoholic who can no longer drink yet takes pleasure in watching others indulge. His untroubled snores, the comfort he took in the garbage truck he slept with, like a teddy bear, was to me a sort of perfection, a state of grace I feared I'd destroy if I wasn't careful.

One such night, hidden in the dark of his room, I was transported back to a Pittsburgh VA hospital, the summer I was thirteen. It was before I had a son of my own, before Dominic's HIV, before my own war, and my father lay in bed asleep, recovering from surgery to remove the tumor that would eventually kill him, from Agent Orange. He was on morphine, which at the time I knew nothing of, except what I'd seen in movies, where you'd get jabbed and your troubles melted away, almost like magic. But morphine (like most things, I've discovered) isn't "as advertised." A *motherfucker*, as my Marines might say.

At first, it was just a glassy look. Some confusion. My father would ask to call people on the phone. His mother, dead for years. Uncle Eddie, gone as well. He'd even ask to call me, though I was standing next to him. And when we'd dial, he'd become distracted by an address book or one of the laminated photographs of us he'd carried in his wallet—worried that he'd lost them. He'd search his hospital gown, inside his pillow case, absurd places—and when finally we'd locate whatever he was looking for, he wouldn't recognize it.

One day, while we visited, Mom and Dominic went to look at books in the hospital library. My father dozed as, on a TV mounted to the wall, I watched *Felix the Cat*—a mad scientist plotted to steal Felix's magic bag.

My father began talking in his sleep. No words really, more like groans, or whimpering, a dog whining to be let out. Annoyed, I turned the TV louder. Felix's mad scientist begged the universe—*I must know what's inside that bag!*—and pulled at the hair crowning his head, like it burned. My father moaned, louder now—an unsettling reminder of just how close the worlds of the living and dead were. His eyes popped open with a *whoosh*, startling me, like heat from a bonfire being lit.

"Daddy?" I asked, checking to see if anyone had heard, embarrassed I still called him "Daddy" at thirteen. He didn't react. Maybe he was still asleep, I thought, dreaming with his eyes open.

My father reached for me, grasping and frantic, as if being pulled away. I stumbled back, afraid I'd done something wrong. Not knowing what to do, I hugged him, apologizing. My father, still powerful despite the poisons that'd claimed his body, lifted me from the floor and bound me to him, desperate, like a drowning man. For the first time, his arms terrified me—not for their fearsome strength, something I'd always envied and obeyed, but for the furious love they possessed.

"Francis," he said with startling sadness, "take cover. Please . . ." I tried soothing him. Told him he was a good dad. That I loved him. He took my face in his hands, looked at me, and whispered *"Mortars,"* as if sharing a terrible secret.

"The bunker," he pleaded. "Get in the bunker." He ripped at the tubes binding him, tendrils of plastic seemingly repossessing his body, like kudzu vines strangling an abandoned house. I pressed my thirteen-year-old self, barely 120 pounds of bone and not much muscle, against him. He fought, begging me to take cover in the bunker that would shelter us from the mortars.

I felt a tear.

And then more, like a ditch flooding after a storm, sweeping away everything, a kind of a blessing, heartbroken and fierce on my face. I knew in that moment he was giving me permission to surrender. To let go.

Yet I held to him, buried my face, and sobbed, as deep within my father, I heard something swelling, primal and lonely and full of sorrow, wild to be free.

In that moment, I would have gladly died with him.

And in the quiet of that moment, no more than a breath really, I felt his body tremble, as in a seizure. I was thrown from him. From the floor, I watched my father tumble from bed, blood streaming from his hands, where the tubes had been. He threw himself on me, shielding me, as above us, Felix's mad scientist lamented his doom, unable to control the bag's terrible magic.

A commercial came on.

My father lay on top of me, repeating my name. And, strangely to me at the time, he asked for forgiveness until his body slowly surrendered and he grew quiet, as if succumbing to a kind of peace, maybe similar to what the kamikaze experienced before plunging into the deck of Uncle Eddie's ship.

It was the closest I'd ever felt to him.

Is it ever possible to know someone? To know what's inside? Who knows who my father was? What his true feelings were—about me, our family, our life? What sins did he struggle with? But in that moment, as he lay on top of me, I knew I was his son.

Before he died, not quite twelve years after that, my father couldn't stand on his own. As I helped him from bed, to see Mom and Dominic waving from below, on the frost-burned hospital lawn, my father asked where he should be buried. It was an admission that we'd reached the end. That what needed to be said needed to be said now. He clung to me, an arm wrapped around my shoulders. I held his once sure hand, my arm barely reaching across his yet broad back.

I didn't answer. I didn't want to talk about it.

"What about Arlington? Or Quantico?" he asked, referring to the national cemeteries. "They'd do it for free."

"Sure," I finally agreed. "Sounds good, Daddy." I wanted him to stop talking.

As we struggled to the window, our future measured now in footsteps, he said, "Maybe you just went further than me."

His statement, though simple, possessed an undeniable truthfulness that caught me by surprise. His distillation of our lives, our relationship, almost twenty-five years now, into one statement, seven words, haunted me—evidence that he was already transiting to what's "next," and therefore in possession of a rare wisdom.

I didn't answer.

Thank You for Your Service . . . Sucker!

Thank you for your service.

I'd heard it hundreds, maybe even thousands, of times, since leaving the Corps. I'd always responded with *You're welcome* or some other equally bland response, a verbal placeholder. They mean well, these grateful Americans, but have no idea. Their impression of my time in the Marines comes mostly from movies and TV—Jack Nicholson bellowing *You can't handle the truth!* on a Hollywood witness stand, a reworking of the King Arthur "Sword in the Stone" legend in a recruiting commercial, the uniquely American promise of "transformation" realized. Or at a ball game, as some old guy in a wheelchair is rolled out like a museum exhibit, choking on the dust of oblivion, as the organ plays the "Marines' Hymn." He waves, the crowd dutifully gets to its feet, cheering. The franchise loves it, adding as it does an implied meaning, a touch of grace to an otherwise graceless commerce, a wolfish buying and selling in sheep's clothing. But what does the old vet get out of it? Was it worth it for him?

Some context is in order. As a former lieutenant of Marines and veteran of the righteous wrong known as the Persian Gulf War, I'm not in a wheelchair (yet), but I do have ulcerative colitis (mild to severe, says the doc) and tinnitus so bad that it's made me see the upside of a bullet to the head. (With my luck, even a bullet wouldn't stop the ringing.) Sleep apnea, too.

And so, they thank me. At first, it was touching. A crocheted lei from a first grader at a Honolulu elementary school as we stepped off the plane from the Gulf. A six-pack on the sly from a sympathetic bartender in Eau Claire, Wisconsin. A medal from a grateful foreign nation, one that now sits in my garage, beneath a broken microwave, old tax returns, and mildewy camping gear. In my darker moments, I sometimes wonder if the "gold" is real—and how much I might get if I sold it. I've seen them before, in cardboard boxes at yard sales and flea markets—I wouldn't get much. But why make me stoop to that? Just write me a check. They certainly could afford it—I made them a lot of money. Because, ultimately, that's what it's about: *money.* It was always transactional— my service to this country. The medals are merely a romantic attempt to suggest otherwise. So when they thank me, these Americans, maybe it's just a smoke screen for their complicity, their guilt.

I think about this as my father, the Marine pilot, with his own medals from grateful nations, lies marooned— eighty-sixed, done for—in a bed at Bethesda Naval Hospital. I've spent the past two months soothing him with wet washcloths, wiping his ass as navy corpsmen, half his age, roll him on his side like cowhands branding a bull, and massaging his still powerful legs—the pillars of a ruined temple. And when I stop, hands aching, he moans— *begs*—that I continue. He's fifty-six. And won't be coming home.

I just want it to be over.

As I do my best to ignore him, to escape, even momentarily—my father, his cancer, this hospital room—my phone rings. A collection agent. He's all business. Skips right to the unpleasantries. My deadbeat status has rendered all small talk void, civility canceled like a bad debt. He grills me about my overdue cell bill, lectures me on fiscal responsibility, my duties as a good American. After a few moments, I tell him of *the bill*—a now infamous phone bill—that cost a month's pay, as I called home from the Saudi desert. Like a forensic accountant testifying before a grand jury, I do a painstaking recitation of the twenty-nine-year-old bill, a kind of clerical torture, even remembering the exact dollar amount—$1,385.56 (1991 dollars, I remind him). He's confused, but that's all part of it—the muddying of the waters, pitting his patriotism against his capitalism.

"Thank you for your service, Mr. Keane, but . . ."

"I want a new cell phone," I cut him off. "The one made out of titanium. I like the way that sounds, *titanium*, like a weapon. Free cell service too. For life. And a monthly stipend. Beer money, say . . . $500? Adjusted yearly, of course, for inflation."

There's a pause. He's checking his script presumably. In the silence, I offer salvation, a way out: "Look. I'm a reasonable man. A disabled veteran. A fellow patriot, y'know—a free-market capitalist. So I'll cut you a break. Just send that beer money and I'll let you slide," and then hang up before he can resume his good-citizenship lesson. The smoke screen works both ways—it's for me to disappear behind as well.

Since then, I've kept an informal tally—a dollar amount on how much my service was worth—and whether it balanced out the true cost. Losing thirty pounds when I didn't have thirty pounds to lose. Being admitted to the hospital when the urgent-care doctor shuddered and said: *You looked wasted, bro.* The clumps of hair. The blood. The looks on my kids' faces as they realized I might not be around to see them grow up, or have their own kids. *It's just a nagging condition,* I assure them. But maybe it's not? Maybe I won't live that long. And the scary thing? That thought is actually comforting.

There's an inscription on the back of that medal, the one from the grateful nation, written in Arabic. I'm afraid to have it translated for fear it says: *Thank you for your service . . . sucker!*

But nobody joined the Marines to get rich. I knew that going in. I wanted transformation. I wanted to be a *Marine*—like my father. Like Brawley.

I remember Brawley. *Carl.* How he bear hugged me when I found out Dominic was HIV positive and dying. Didn't say anything, just hugged me. Because he *knew.* After his memorial service, I carried Brawley in his box, California sun streaming through Iwo Jima flag-raising stained-glass windows at the Camp Pendleton chapel, to

be loaded into his truck along with boot-camp graduation pictures and leftover Costco cake. I hugged Evangeline, his wife, remembering how she'd fed me *gallo pinto*,
Costa Rican rice and beans, after a long night drinking,
Carl passed out on their couch. Evangeline was a mother
to me when my own wouldn't, even though she was only
a few years older.

I remember Gibbs. His fiftieth birthday in Acres
Homes, North Houston, drinking beer and shit talking
playing bones in the backyard. I take great comfort knowing a seat awaits me at their family table, heavy with pork
chops, gumbo, and homemade *boudin* sausage—fat with
Gulf shrimp, oysters, and crab. *Francis don't eat like your
other white friends*, Miss Rita said. *Aww, Mom! Why you
gotta do the lieutenant like that?* Gibbs laughed. A seat in
the pew, though I don't believe in God anymore, at least
not in a god created by men. A Busch tallboy waiting in
the garage refrigerator on a humid H-Town day, ice chips
making a humble can of beer seem like an indulgence,
"the water of life," like Irish whiskey, as I sat with Mr.
G—listening to staticky blues on the radio and child-rear-
ing wisdom—as he, retired from two jobs, now raised his
grandchildren. He offered me a place to hide out, to disappear, should the need ever arise, no questions asked.
*You stay in my house, under my roof, eat my food, drink my
beer. You just show up. I'll take you in.*

I remember Harris. My son worked his farm in Alabama last summer. Slopped hogs. Dug holes. Went
hunting. Hoping some of that Harris grit, that *magic*—
that made cigarettes defy gravity—would rub off on my

LA kid. When I went to pick him up, we got drunk on moonshine strained through a "clean Hanes undershirt" into an empty handle of Captain Morgan, how they do it in Shelby County. (Harris is a Glenlivet eighteen-year man. The moonshine was my request, a nod to the romance in my blood.) As we drank, we were surrounded by the Harris family, if only in the framed photographs of the departed—his father, brothers, cousins, uncles, grandfathers—all wearing the uniform of the US military. Harris's family, and thousands of others, have borne our nation's burden since Crispus Attucks caught the first bullet at the Boston Massacre. Harris even ends each phone call with an unapologetic "I love you."

And what did I do to deserve such love? Maybe because we *suffered* together, and that bound us.

So if colitis, sleep apnea, and tinnitus are the price to be a member of this tribe, then—so be it. Because it was never about money. It was about *transformation*—just not the way the TV commercials promised.

You're welcome.

Some of us think holding on makes us strong, but sometimes it is letting go.
—Hermann Hesse

Brian O'Hare is a graduate of the US Naval Academy and former US Marine Corps officer. His career began in a Baltimore bar, the legendary Club Charles, where director John Waters cast him to appear in his film *Cry Baby*. Currently, he's an award-winning writer and filmmaker living in Los Angeles. His work has appeared in *War, Literature and the Arts*; *Santa Fe Writers Project*; *Hobart*; and other journals, and he has been nominated for two Pushcart Prizes. He was named a Writing Fellow at the Virginia Center for the Creative Arts and served as Visiting Writer at CUNY/ Kingsborough (Brooklyn). He's currently at work on his debut novel.